Early Praise f‹

"Defiant is a book that will make you
also make you cheer for its protagonis‹
compliance to defiance, from heteronormative and allistic performance
to honesty and inner strength, is narrated in clear, stunning, and
revelatory language."

> — N.I. Nicholson, author of *Novena (remixed)* and
> Editor-in-Chief of *Barking Sycamores*

"In Defiant, Michael Scott Monje Jr. has created an authentic portrait
of life as an autistic adult. The questions that Clay Dillon struggles with
in the wake of his diagnosis—questions of disability, mental health and
gender identity—will be familiar to autistic readers, especially those
diagnosed as adults.

Michael deftly navigates Clay's exploration of the shifting boundaries of
disclosure and his struggles to balance his personal and professional
lives, bringing both insight and unflinching honesty to the narrative.
While Defiant is part of the Clay Dillon series, it works equally as well
as a stand alone novel."

> — Cynthia Kim, author of *I Think I Might Be Autistic*
> and *Nerdy, Shy, and Socially Innappopriate*

"For many of us a late-in-life autism diagnosis asks as many questions as
it answers. *Defiant* takes a bare bones approach in speaking to readers
from that very angle.

Monje drops us like a bomb in the thick of things and yells, "Go!"
Clay Dillon, a newly diagnosed adult coming to terms with what being
disabled means on both personal and professional levels is such a
realistic and relatable character, and Monje writes him beautifully. I'm
in!"

> — S.R. Salas, author of *Black and White: A Colorful
> Look at Life on the Autism Spectrum*

Other works by Michael Scott Monje, Jr.:

Novels

Nothing is Right

Mirror Project

Electronic Chapbooks

A Waking Narrative

Defiant

Michael Scott Monje, Jr.

Owned by disabled workers, Autonomous Press
seeks to revolutionize academic access.

Autonomous Press is an independent publisher focusing on works about disability, neurodivergence, and the various ways they can intersect with other aspects of identity and lived experience.

ISBN-10: 0986183504

ISBN-13: 978-0-9861835-0-8

Clay Dillon and the *Shaping Clay* series are an ongoing artistic project by Michael Scott Monje, Jr. Their related works are fictional, and the subject matter is not meant to depict any actual persons or their actions, living or dead.

For more information about the series, or to see the currently serialized episodes, visit **http://www.mmonjejr.com**.

Foreword by Nick Walker

Last time we met Clay Dillon, he was six years old and nothing was right.

If you haven't already read *Nothing Is Right*, Mike Monje's first Clay Dillon novel, that's okay. *Defiant* takes place 23 years later, and it works more or less equally well to start with the six-year-old Clay and then read *Defiant* to see what the little guy's future holds, or to start with the 30-year-old Clay and then go back to discover where he came from. (And even as I write these words, Monje is already well into the writing of the next Clay Dillon novel, *Imaginary Friends*, which takes us back again to Clay's childhood, picking up not long after *Nothing Is Right* left off.)

Like Monje, Clay Dillon is autistic. The young Clay of *Nothing Is Right* didn't know he was autistic, and the adults around him didn't know it either. *Defiant* begins just after Clay has finally found out. At the age of 30.

Imagine spending your entire childhood, adolescence, and young adulthood knowing that you're different from everyone else in your world—different from your family, your teachers, your peers, the people you pass on the street. Not different in the superficial ways that elementary school teachers and "inspirational" writers are talking about when they repeat cutesy platitudes about how everyone is special. Different in the fundamental workings of your mind. Different in the ways you experience, use, and understand language. Different in the ways you perceive reality—not just differences of viewpoint, but differences in basic sensory experience, differences between what you see, hear, and feel, and what everyone else claims to be seeing, hearing, and feeling. Different in ways that make understanding between yourself and the people around you impossible, because on a basic neurobiological level, they're incapable of experiencing anything like the reality you experience, and you're incapable of experiencing anything like the reality they experience. They don't understand what your thought processes are like, or your emotions, or the reasons behind most of your actions, and you don't understand any of those things about them, either.

And imagine that because these people who are so vastly different from you also vastly outnumber you, all of the constant confusions and difficulties that stem from these differences are blamed on you—

attributed to some failing, deficiency, bad intent, or general wrongness on your part. They're different from you and you're different from them, but the way they tell the story, the way the story is taught to you, is that they are normal, and normal means good and right, and you're not normal, which means you're bad and wrong. At best, most people respond to you with puzzlement or pity; more often, with hostility, cruelty, or contempt. And no matter how hard you try to change this state of affairs (and you try harder than any of them will ever know), no matter what you do, nothing is right.

And imagine that you have no name for what it is that sets you apart from others, no name for the nature of the difference.

And then one day you find out that there *is* a name for it.

After 30 fucking years.

Having a name for it means that suddenly you have a way to start talking about it. The name means a new understanding, a new lens through which your past and present can be seen in an entirely new way. The name is a starting point from which you can begin to create a new and coherent narrative from the chaos of your life. A starting point for communication and understanding between yourself and others, about who you are, how you and they might differ, how you can work together. A starting point for finding other people like yourself, reading what they've written, benefitting from their experience, joining with them in communities of mutual support. A starting point for the task of discovering what you really need in order to have a better life, a life that fits you, a life in which some things, sometimes, can finally be right.

At the same time, it's a bit of a shock. As the old saying goes, "The truth will set you free, but first it will make you miserable." The radical shift in self-perception that comes from discovering in adulthood that one is autistic can be profoundly disorienting. And the cascade of insights that flow from such a discovery, however valuable and transformative in the long run, may be accompanied by intense anger and grief. As Monje explained in an introductory post when he first began publishing *Defiant* in serial form on his blog, Shaping Clay:

> In Clay's case, as in my own, the grief is not so much a matter of feeling like a limitation has been imposed, and it's definitely not the feeling that the diagnosis somehow diminishes us as people. Instead, it's grief for the childhood and younger adulthood that he could have had—a grief for the

opportunities lost, if only we had been properly supported and taught.

So Clay is in a fragile state right now, as this chapter of his saga begins. While he's finally discovered he's autistic, he has very little idea of what this really means, or can be made to mean, in the context of his actual life. Mostly he's flailing around trying to cope, as his old understanding of who he is crumbles around him. And to top it all off, he's about to make the all-too-common mistake of putting himself in the hands of a non-autistic psychologist.

Clay and the psychologist, Dr. Williams, live in two different worlds. I hold citizenship in both worlds, which might be why I got the job of writing this foreword. I'm autistic, and I also have an academic career which consists to a large extent of teaching psychology to students who are headed for careers in psychotherapy and related professions.

When I read *Defiant* through my autistic eyes, Dr. Williams is the book's villain. I've seen too many people harmed by the Dr. Williamses of the world, the condescending "experts" whose "expert knowledge" consists of a steaming heap of stereotypes, prejudices, and unsound theories and practices invented by other non-autistic "experts."

But when I read *Defiant* through the eyes of a teacher of psychology, Dr. Williams seems more tragic than malign. She was probably drawn to the field of psychotherapy by the same thing that draws most of the aspiring therapists who show up in my classes: a genuine interest in human beings and in helping human beings to make positive changes in their lives. And somewhere along the way, she got lost in all her acquired expertise, and in the comforting illusion of certainty and superiority that such expertise conveys. And now she's face-to-face with a fascinating, unique, beautiful human being who's primed to begin an extraordinary process of transformation... and her head is so stuffed with expertise that she can't see him.

I'll be recommending *Defiant* to my fellow autistics for many reasons, and one reason is that it serves as a cautionary tale that might save some readers from "experts" like Dr. Williams. I'll also be assigning *Defiant* to my psychology students, in the hopes that it will save them from *becoming* Dr. Williams.

But enough about Dr. Williams. Let me say a bit more about Clay.

D.W. Winnicott, a pioneer in the field of child psychology who was quite a bit wiser than Dr. Williams, said that when children grow up in environments in which it's unsafe to express their true selves, they develop "false selves" that are in closer compliance with what's demanded of them. By the time they reach adulthood they may have forgotten that the false self is a mask, donned in compliance with external expectations. The true self is buried, and the mask stays on, however badly it might fit.

With the discovery that he's autistic, the part of Clay's mask that hides his true autistic self (as much from himself as from anyone else) has begun to crumble. But that's not the only part of Clay's false self that's crumbling. The mask is cracking all over. That's often how these things go. For instance, Clay's compliance with the dominant societal standards of masculinity is also part of his false self, and that, too, has begun to crack.

And what's underneath? Clay is just starting to find out, and we, the readers, get to find out along with him. Whatever it is, though, it's bound to be infinitely more complex, strange, and beautiful than the ill-fitting mask of compliance. Compliance, as D.W. Winnicott once said, "is a sick basis for life."

And the best antidote to compliance is, of course, defiance.

Nick Walker is an Autistic educator, scholar, and martial artist, as well as an editor at Autonomous Press. He teaches aikido in Berkeley, California, and blogs at Neurocosmopolitanism.com.

A Referral To Dr. Williams

"So, we're here to talk about your autism."

Clay squinted because Dr. Jeannie Williams spoke in such a matter of fact tone that it made her seem hard to look at. "If that's how you want to put it," he replied.

While she watched him, he fidgeted in his chair. It was an uncomfortable chair, but there was no other choice of place for him to sit—Dr. Jeannie Williams occupied the only other seat in the office. Between the discomfort of the chair and Clay's discomfort when calling her "Doctor," there was no controlling his squirming. He tried to push the squirms down his legs until they sat below his knee, where he could work them out by flexing and releasing his calves, but that did not work. They were too big today; there was no way they would fit below his knees like they usually did.

It seemed strange to him that he was having such a hard time calling her "Doctor." He worked in academia, and most of his colleagues had doctorates. Most of them were also his superiors, so he was used to calling non-medical doctors "Doctor." He decided that his problem was that she would be treating him as a patient, and yet she had not been to medical school. It was one thing to call an English or Philosophy professor "Doctor"—they did not purport to know whether he was healthy or ill. A psychologist, on the other hand, lived in a dangerous place. A psychologist could be licensed to treat him; even to issue him prescriptions, maybe; and yet, that psychologist did not necessarily need to take the same classes in biology and organic chemistry that a physician would be required to take before prescribing drugs.

Clay knew that this was one of those things that was just the way the world worked, but it still made him acutely uncomfortable. Why would people do this? Who would support it? It had gotten enough traction as an idea that it had become public policy. How did that happen?

Clay did not necessarily feel like Dr. Williams was his enemy, but he did feel like policies that created this much discomfort for him were wrong policies. Since she was benefitting from them, and even helping to perpetuate them, it was hard to see her as an ally. That left her in the same kind of wary middle ground that he put strangers on the street into, except that he was supposed to be seeing her for treatment.

Could he trust the treatment? Even if it was recommended by an underqualified person who was taking advantage of bad policies? That was a hard question. Especially since he had no other choice—Dr. Jeannie Williams was his last chance. The previous two referrals he had obtained from the county's mental health people had been to therapists that were too expensive for him to afford without insurance, and the county's people had been very clear that they could not keep helping him unless he became unemployed again. He just made too much money now.

So, Clay thought, he had to get comfortable with Dr. Jeannie Williams, even if she was more like a doctor of fine arts than a medical professional.

Clay realized that he had been silent for a long time. His face felt hot. He cleared his throat.

"It's not so much that I need to talk about the autism, is what I meant. Actually, knowing that I'm autistic has answered a lot of the questions I used to have about why some things seem to be so hard for me. It's more of the 'what do I do next' that I want help with."

"That makes sense." She smiled. "I've been reviewing the evaluations that were performed when you were seeing the doctors over at the county's Mental Health Services building. I've seen Dr. Wright's diagnosis, and the second opinion from Dr. Naptal backing it up. You seem quite high-functioning, despite what they have to say."

"I don't know what to say to that."

"Why? It's a compliment."

Her eyes danced at him. Clay refused to look at them because he did not want to be distracted by how much Dr. Jeannie Williams was enjoying this encounter. Instead, he looked at the ceiling while he talked.

"I don't know what to say because I don't know how to take a compliment that isn't a compliment. I don't want to call you a liar, but it doesn't seem very 'high-functioning' to me to be thirty and to never have worked a full-time job. It doesn't feel like I'm 'high-functioning' when I need six months of therapy to build up the skills to convince my alma mater that I am qualified to teach the subject they gave me a degree in. Instead, it kind of feels like you're saying that I'm not worth your time, and that you don't know how to treat me."

Dr. Williams leaned back in her seat and tapped her knee with her pen. Clay wondered if she was stimming, or if she was just working off some aggression because she did not like being contradicted.

"Okay. I can see where you're coming from," the tone of her voice was still light. "Would you prefer if I said 'Asperger's'?"

Clay shook his head. "That's not what Dr. Naptal said. He said I was autistic."

Dr. Williams smiled, but Clay was pretty sure that she was not happy. He had no idea why, but he felt like she was yelling at him even though her words were very light and her sentences trailed upward at the end. He dug his thumbnails into the meat of his index fingers. The short spike of pain calmed him down.

"People with Asperger's Syndrome are autistic," Dr. Williams said. "They just don't have quite the same presentation of symptoms that we see in more severely autistic children. For instance, they are usually quite verbal, like you are. They also tend to have higher IQs."

Clay dug his thumbnails into this index fingers again. "If that's what I am, then you can call me that. Did Dr. Naptal and Dr. Wright make a mistake?"

"Not really. They might have underestimated your outcomes, that's all. People with Aspergers tend to have a better chance at being employable, and you've shown that you're employable. They still have trouble with long-term relationships, though, which was why I was surprised to hear that you are in a marriage that has lasted for over a decade. That's quite the accomplishment."

Clay twisted in his seat. Something was not right here. Dr. Williams was not acting like the county doctors had acted. They had wanted to know what he wanted and how he felt. They had not pronounced judgments about the way he lived his life.

He did not know how to respond to Dr. Williams's assessments. Was he failing to see his behavior from her point of view? Or was she overstepping her bounds and making assumptions that she did not have a right to make?

Clay took a deep breath. Dr. Wright had referred him to Dr. Williams after all. Maybe this was just the next phase. Maybe the reason that Dr. Wright and Dr. Naptal had not been very prescriptive was because they were working on diagnosis, not treatment. They had said that Dr. Williams was a behavior specialist. If that was true, then she was probably describing his behavior back to him so that he could know how it would be perceived by others. If she said that he was not going to have very much trouble, then maybe it was a good thing.

"So," Dr. Williams crossed her legs and bounced her pen on her knee again. "Let's talk about employment. What makes you so concerned with your employment status now? Why wasn't this ringing bells for you at, say, twenty or twenty-five?"

"Well," Clay said, "I spent my early twenties building up a freelance graphic design business. I wasn't trying to work for other people, so I didn't know that I would have such a hard time with it. It wasn't until Noahleen—that's my wife's name—"

"I have it here in the records," Dr. Williams broke in.

"—Okay. It wasn't until Noahleen got sick that I even had to find full time employment. Before that, we had an agreement: she'd work the day job while I built up my business, and then when it got to be big enough that I wanted to hire employees, she would quit and work with me. I kept getting close. For a while, I was even making more money than her. I just never got quite enough work to justify her quitting her job and working for me. Then she started to have seizures."

"How long ago was this?"

"This was about four or five years ago."

"So this was still a long time ago. How have you managed to get her access to her treatment for so long? And why did you only just seek help last year?"

Clay fidgeted. He was sure that this stuff was all in the notes. Why did he have to repeat himself so much when he dealt with medical professionals? Did they have trouble reading their own records?

"Well, when Noahleen got really sick, I was making enough to get us by on COBRA for a while. When her seizures got too bad, though, the plan dropped us. They said she had exceeded a lifetime cap. I had to help her get on Medicaid and Medicare before we could afford her surgery. Then, when things got too crazy and I couldn't do that much freelance work because I was with her in the hospital, we moved back in with her folks for a while. They didn't really expect me to work until she was in the clear.

"By the time she was stable, I realized that I didn't want to work for a big company that was going to need me to be out of the house a lot. I had also lost most of my clients by then. I'd just been away from the profession for too long, and I didn't have the time to build my network back up. Noahleen and I agreed then that I would go back for my Master's, so that I could teach. She had a little coming in from disability, so even if my income got too high for us to keep on with Medicaid, she'd still have enough money to pay her co-pays.

"Graduate school was good, too. I had insurance again, real insurance, through the student union. Teaching agreed with me. I even won an award for it. Then, when I graduated, I couldn't get a job. I applied to over forty different institutions, and I got a handful of interviews, but I never got an offer or even a personal call back. I couldn't get anyone to look at me for part time positions either. I did what I was supposed to do, but the only jobs I could get were light industrial gigs through a temp agency.

"So, one day, after my alma mater had even turned me down for a part time teaching job, Noahleen said to me that maybe it was me. Maybe I should go talk to somebody, because maybe I just didn't know how to work for other people. By that time, we were able to get out of her parents' house and into a shitty little apartment, but if I couldn't hold down work then we were going to go broke and have to move back in with them again. That was when I went down to the county building. It wasn't even that I thought I needed the free doctors or anything, it was more because I didn't know of any other place to go. Back when my mom was in and out of institutions, the county building was always where she'd end up, so I just went there.

"It turns out that was the right choice, though, because I found out later how expensive it can be to see a psychiatrist without insurance. I always knew therapy was expensive, because back when I was growing up, my dad's insurance didn't cover it, so I thought it was just something I'd have to pay for. I didn't realize how different it was if you talked to a doctor though, instead of a therapist."

Dr. Williams nodded along with Clay as he narrated his background to her. She did not take notes. Clay assumed that she must be recording everything.

"So your partner, she's still too disabled to work?" Dr. Williams asked.

Clay nodded. "She's doing better than she was, but to keep her seizures under control they had to put her on so many drugs that she sleeps most of the day. I don't think she's ever going back to work."

"That's too bad."

Clay nodded.

"Okay, so... if you had to state your goals in one short statement, what would you say?"

Clay did not know how to answer the question. He had a lot of goals. He wanted to be able to teach full-time, or at least to teach half-time and while rebuilding his graphic design business. He wanted to understand why Noahleen always acted like she was afraid of him when he got angry. He wanted to know if he was going to wind up schizophrenic like his mother, or if the autism would protect him from that. And he wanted to know if his Grandpa Harry had actually been crazy or if he had also been autistic.

Clay knew that this would all be too much for Dr. Williams to understand right away, so he did not know what to tell her. He stayed silent instead.

"Come on, Clay," she said. "If you had to name one thing that you want to work on first, what would it be?"

Clay thought for a moment. Then he said, "I want to understand what people are asking me when they ask questions, and I'd like them to understand my answers."

Dr. Williams nodded. "That sounds reasonable. Let's talk about how we're going to do that."

For the rest of the session, Clay listened while Dr. Williams outlined her plans for his short-term goal. Most of it seemed to revolve around exercises and games that they would use to talk about his presentation socially. None of her ideas centered on vocabulary or self-expression, though—they all seemed to focus on building up his ability to resist the urge to fidget, or to endure prolonged eye contact.

When she started talking about her plans for their next meeting, he dug his fingernails into the palms of his hands to keep himself from interrupting her. Then he started to count the number of seconds until she told him that he was free to go for the day.

❖ ❖ ❖

Reflecting on Regrets

Clay stared at himself in the mirror while he let the sink run hot water over his razor. It was hard for him to not believe that the mirror stared back. He thought about the things that Dr. Williams said during their encounter, and about his discomfort during their meeting.

Not that she said anything in particular to make him feel the way he did. Instead, she seemed to want to channel the conversation along certain lines, and having her dictate the terms of his treatment to him in such an explicit way, that had been uncomfortable. Clay had always been under the impression that therapy was designed to let the patient talk about what was currently bothering him, and yet Dr. Williams had seemed more concerned with talking about goals and objectives. At first, she had let Clay define those objectives, but as their meeting had progressed, she became more and more prescriptive.

Not that goals and objectives were necessarily bad, he thought as he appraised his own stomach. Goals and objectives had given him visible abs for the first time in his life. He might be stuck at two hundred and eighty pounds, but at least he had muscle to show for it. Just two years ago, his midsection had been nothing but a sloppy pudge that he had accumulated over the first year of his being a non-smoker. It was just too bad that no one else knew that he had these muscles because they still looked like a beer belly when he had a shirt on.

Clay knew that he would need to bulk up his chest and shoulders if he wanted to make his proportions right, but he did not want to gain any more weight because his knees already hurt more often than not.

Goals and objectives were fine. But, Clay thought, it would also be fine to talk about the things he wanted but could not have. For instance, he wanted to get his weight down to two hundred pounds again. He knew it was unrealistic to expect that to happen, but he wanted it.

He had been two hundred pounds when he was twenty-five. He had been two hundred pounds, and he had been able to wear tight jeans, and he had even put on Noahleen's hip huggers once or twice and belted them off with one of her sequined belts. He had been thin enough that people just accepted it. They might not have liked it, but... so what?

It was just like when he was in high school, and he had been dating mostly girls, mostly from the city's magnet school for gifted kids. Those were girls that did not mind if he was more comfortable in a leather skirt than in the combat BDUs he wore to his own high school out in the suburbs.

Of course, he had worn the leather skirts before his beard had fully come in. And before he had developed back hair.

What was it, he wondered, about being nude in front of a mirror? It always made him remember the things he had left behind.

That was the kind of topic he wanted to be able to bring up with Dr. Williams, but he got the sense that she would not be so receptive to talking about his body. She might try to push him to set goals, like those hard-sell assholes at the gym did. Or she might think he was a pervert. Most other people had. Even the ones that he never told about his penchant for skirts. Noahleen's mom had accused him of being a cross-dresser when they got engaged, and he had not even tried on a skirt in four or five years by that point. Somehow she had just read it on his face.

Thinking about his face reminded Clay why he was there, in the bathroom. As he lathered himself up with shaving gel, he could not help noticing the way his neck had thickened with age. It was something he rarely paid attention to, but when he did, it made him sad. It was the final nail in the coffin for that teenager in the leather skirt and fishnet stockings.

Well, he might not be able to make himself thin enough to feel good in a dress, but he could at least keep himself looking young. A good shave could do that—it could tame his five o'clock shadow well enough to keep him looking like a boy who only had to shave twice a week. It was not the kind of beauty he wanted, but it was the kind he could have. The kind that would not look too out of place on a two hundred and eighty pound man with abs.

He bent himself forward and stuck his ass out, another thing he knew better than to do in public. At least, now. Years of being called a faggot for carrying himself in a way that was comfortable to him had taught him how people expected him to stand. It put strain on his already bad knees in a way that cocking his weight to one side did not, but it made him look like he was expected to look. It was only here, in private, that he allowed himself to drop his guard and get comfortable.

The mirror was misting up. Clay realized that the bathroom fan was not on, and it was supposed to be.

He cursed himself for skipping a step in the ritual, but he also forgave himself for being distracted because he had been feeling easily distracted ever since his meeting with Dr. Jeannie Williams.

Clay turned the fan on and the faucet down. He would need to wait for a few minutes for the mirror to clear before he could start to shave. While he did, he looked down at his belly. It was not so impressive from above. Just hair and a bulge. The six pack he could see in the mirror did not show itself to the man who had worked so hard to build it.

What if he shaved his body hair again, like he did when he was young? Would it let him feel as good as it had back then? Would it make him less ridiculous if he wanted to wear a skirt? Or did it only feel good back then because it let him pretend that his childhood was a little longer, and that he could dam up the changes that were rocking his body until he *chose* to experience them?

Had he been expressing his real self, or playing dress-up?

Clay knew that deep down, the answer was there, but he purposefully stopped looking for it. There was too much, now, that would be affected by such a big change in the way he interacted with the world. He had to think about how his actions would affect Noahleen. How they would affect his future employment. What her family would say.

She had never even spoken to her parents about the fact that she had been involved exclusively with women all through high school. How could he ask her to advocate for him, when she had never really come out of her own closet?

More importantly, how could he split his attention between advocating for his needs as a person with autism and standing up for his right to wear whatever he wanted, no matter what anyone else thought?

If he looked like he had just a few years ago, then he might be willing to try. Now, though…

Now he would only make himself look ridiculous.

No one wants to see a heavyweight wrestler in a dress, and Clay accepted that as what everyone else would see if he tried to break free of their expectations for him. Some things just had to belong to the past. He was thirty now, so it was time to accept that and to focus on the things he would need to do in order to provide for himself and for Noahleen.

That was probably what Dr. Williams had been focused on, he realized. And maybe, once she saw that he was working on the same thing, she would be more open to helping him process these feelings. For now, he would keep himself looking young. He could at least do that. It would give him an advantage, too, he thought. If he looked young, at least people would not question why his resume was so short.

Clay picked up the razor and leaned forward, resting his belly and his left hip on the counter top. His old fashioned Merkur was heavy, and he had loaded it with a fresh Iridium blade. He would need to be careful as he worked, to make sure he only carved away the pieces of himself that he no longer needed.

❖ ❖ ❖

Exercising Restraint

Clay watched Noahleen twist underneath him as she searched for his body. She kept trying to reach out for him even though her wrists were tied tightly to her ankles, which were held apart by the spreader bar. He liked this part best, especially since she had her eyes covered.

Her eyes were the windows to his soul. When she could not stare him down, she also could not take control away from him. When he slipped the blindfold over her and he tied her wrists to the ankle loops on the spreader, then she had to trust him to make the decisions for both of them. She had to allow that even though he was mostly useless when it came to chatting up strangers, he knew the subtle signals that she threw off constantly while he was inside of her.

And he did. He knew them all, and he could close his eyes and hear her speak to him through his fingertips. It was louder and more clear when it was her belly, her thighs, or her neck muscles that were forced to do the talking, but any place he touched would eventually start to tell him what he needed to know about whether she was comfortable or not, whether he was being too gentle or too rough, and where he should go next. Her muscles told his fingers this story faster than she could talk.

Her anticipation drew her taut.

Clay watched her lips contort, and then seek, and then curl angrily as she searched for his body on the bed. He would sometimes let her brush up against his hand or his thigh. Mostly, though, he would touch her for a while, massage her, feel her warm up, and then take himself away so to watch her twist herself around as she looked for him. No matter how often they played this game, she never seemed to guess that he was not in bed with her, but standing over it, watching and occasionally giving her false clues by touching just her left thigh or by teasing her stomach with just one finger.

Sometimes, he wanted to push further. Sometimes, she begged him to, pleading for him to slap her or to put clamps on her nipples. Once or twice, they'd talked about what it would mean for him to have license to push her further, even to get into choking or electric prods. They never pushed it further than conversation, though.

Clay knew that there were limits to that rougher kind of play— times it could sour because a cue was missed, or a boundary was not crossed but a trigger was pulled anyway. He preferred to play the game of anticipation instead. He would not attempt to push Noahleen—that would be risky, since stress and persistent pain could both bring on her seizures. Instead, he gave her constant but ever-rotating deprivation.

She began to whine and to grunt as she attempted to grind her hips at him. It looked silly when she did that because he was not between her legs.

Too silly.

If he did not end this game, then he would start to run the risk that he would laugh at her more than she liked, and that would sour the mood. It was a little disappointing—he had hoped to wear her down until she was too tired to keep begging before he gave in to her. Instead, he had to rush things.

Clay crawled up on the bed and put himself inside Noahleen. She tried again to push herself toward him, but he held her hips in place, keeping her where *he* wanted her to be, until he had been all the way in and then most of the way back out again. He remained just far enough inside her that he would not need to use his hands to reinsert himself. Then he waited.

She twisted and bucked, but he managed to keep her pinned down. She begged and she promised, but he held himself still. He imagined that they were like a bow and a bowstring together—she was flexing under the force of his tension, pulling herself more and more out of shape as he waited until he had enough power built up to—

He pushed himself forward all the way, until he lost himself for a moment and felt like he was part of her. Something hard began grinding away at a part of him that was so far up his torso that he briefly wondered if he had managed to push his entire pelvis into her. She always mistook this move for him being ready to fuck her in earnest, but that was not so. It was actually something he did because she moved against him so much that he was about to lose control, and he needed to change the situation to keep himself from finishing early.

Noahleen screamed, and then she pushed harder than he thought she could. She was pushing him over, and if he failed to do something to take away her leverage, he was going to do a backward somersault off the bed.

Clay pushed his body up off hers until he was only barely touching her, and only in the one place. She screamed. He wished, not for the first time, for a gag. If they used one, though, then he would not get to watch her mouth's gymnastics as she hunted for him in the dark.

Holding himself up on his hands and knees, and refusing to make contact with any part of her body except the part that he was inside, he began to move himself in and out of her. Maintaining this kind of rigidity was exhausting, but the less he allowed her to know about his positioning or his own proximity to finishing, the more she escalated. Finally, when he could no longer feel his arms below the elbows and she had exhausted herself so much that she relaxed into the ropes, he spent himself.

That was not the end of the game, though. He had to be careful what he did with his weight, or he would hurt her by straining her joints too much while they were still limited by the spreader bar. He had to resist his own fatigue. He had to keep himself suspended on his hands and knees until he was able to retreat from the bed. Then he had to release her.

That was the truly frustrating part. Standing there, sticky and tired and wanting to collapse into the mattress that was right beneath both of them, but not being able to. Having to pick at the knots that she'd pulled tighter than she was supposed to be able to. Making sure that she was good, that there was nothing else she needed from him.

Before they'd played these games, he would make love to her for far longer than she enjoyed, and whether he managed to finish before she got too sore or not would be about as predictable as a coin toss. It was not that either of them was doing anything wrong—it was just the sheer chaos that came from having so many touches and so many limbs and not being able to tell a touch on his ankle from a touch on his chin from…

Noahleen tore the blindfold off herself. Her eyes blinked wide, expanding as if they were gulping down air after a long time underwater. Now that she was free, Clay collapsed onto the bed and rolled onto his back to watch the ceiling fan.

"So, when are you going to let me hold you down and have *my* way with *you?*"

Noahleen's question sounded innocent, but Clay knew if he looked at her, there would be mischief in the corners of her eyes.

He sneered because he knew it would make her laugh. "You hold me down and have your way with me all the time. I deserve to be the boss for half an hour each week."

She snorted. "When was the last time I made you do things my way—I mean really made you? Like, to the same extreme degree that you just forced me to be still and to wait for you to decide what happens?"

"Hmmm…" Clay paused until the space between them tightened and took on the thickness of silk rope. "How about every time your parents call and invite us to a party that's happening the next day? We always cancel everything to go eat pulled pork in someone's backyard."

She jumped on him, straddling his chest. The way her breasts swung over him was slightly terrifying.

"Not fair," she said. "I don't like going to those parties either."

Clay tried to heave her over, to unseat her and turn the control back over to himself. He had no leverage, though. She was sitting too high on his chest.

"What's wrong?" she asked.

He refused to answer. Instead, he tried again to heave her off.

"Keep doing that," she said, "it feels good. Wait." She ground her pelvis down on him. It felt like one of his ribs was going to crack. "There. Like that. Now try to fight me off. You're in just the right spot."

"What the fuck?"

She giggled. "Now fight me." She slapped him. Not hard, but she slapped him. "I said fight me."

He did. He popped his hips and tried to snap himself upright, but she pushed down on his chest until he could not draw a breath. After a few seconds, black spots appeared at the corners of his vision, and Clay found himself lacking the strength to try to unseat her again.

She slipped off him and padded around to the other side of the bed. Clay wanted to sit up and say something, but his arms and legs were tingling too much. Instead, he listened as she gathered her clothes and slipped off to the bathroom, closing the door behind herself.

"So, when do I get to have my way?" she asked through the bathroom door. "I think I'd be good at calling the shots. Better than you are, even."

Alone in the dark, Clay admitted to himself that she was probably right.

He wondered if he should talk to her about the things he contemplated in the mirror while he shaved. It seemed like it would be pointless for him to bring them up to Dr. Williams. She only wanted to talk about how he acted, not what he felt like. If Noahleen was serious about taking a more dominant and experimental role in their play, then maybe they could use the bedroom to explore some of his feelings.

It would hardly be perfect. Not everything he was feeling came back to sex. Still, it would be a start.

How was he supposed to start that conversation, though? She understood his needs when it came to power exchange, she even shared them. But about this thing—the sense that he had missed something, that he had let his younger self be talked out of doing something that was really more important than it seemed...

He did not even know what he was looking for her to respond to, much less what he hoped that response would be. They had been together for ten years, and right from the start they had been one unit —they had been Clay and Noahleen. It had been so obvious that even after they got married, they still observed the anniversary of their first meeting, and they counted the years of their marriage from that date. Despite that, they had never really talked about, well, about themselves. They had talked about their desires, their goals... they had talked about disability, first when Noahleen started having seizures and then again when Clay was obviously lost in the job market. But them*selves*? The idea that their very identities were not what they appeared to be, that living the default assumptions that other people projected onto them was *optional?* That, they did not discuss.

Not unless it brushed up against sexual orientation, and when that happened, Noahleen tended to embarrass easily. She acted like his occasional and fleeting references to her past relationships were judgments on her, and she was also troubled by his occasional fantasies about other men. She never said anything if he kept it between himself and his pornography, but on the few occasions that he had tried to talk about it, or even just to comment on, say, a particularly attractive actor in a movie, she acted as if he was about to walk out on their relationship.

Knowing that, how was he supposed to talk to her about his desire to... to what? Not to crossdress. More than that. But not necessarily to be a woman, either. He could not see himself keeping it up all the time. It was complicated because it was in-between all the vocabulary that he had for this kind of thing. How was he supposed to find words for it?

He pulled himself up from the bed. It was time to grab a shower and to find out what she wanted to do for dinner. Everything else would have to wait.

❖ ❖ ❖

Noahleen Weighs In

They ate half-dressed, the way that people do when they find themselves in absolute privacy, yet they somehow feel as if there is some special propriety that the dining table demands.

Noahleen had ordered a pizza while Clay was in the shower.

It was all right—no, it was a good pizza—it was just from the same place they always ordered from.

Clay drizzled hot sauce over his slice. It was a procrastination, though, more than a seasoning. The way he slowly drizzled it mirrored the way that he tried to postpone starting up conversation with Noahleen. It was as if nothing could intrude on his attempts to make his pizza just so, and as long as he was still working on the pizza, he did not have to decide whether to talk to Noahleen or not.

Eventually, she broke the silence. She did not do it until after she finished her second slice, but she was the one to do it.

Clay could see that she would be the one to do it well before she spoke. The way that she swallowed the last bite of her pizza and cleaned the corners of her mouth with her napkin told the entire story.

"So, did you want to talk about your first session with Dr. Williams?" she asked. "It's okay if you don't."

He sighed, and his entire body exhaled tension and settled into its seat. Whatever motivated Noahleen to pin him to the bed and demand his submission, it was not something that she was going to discuss. That meant that he would not discuss his own uneasiness with her, or with anyone else for that matter.

"I don't know what to say about her," Clay said. "She seems to have her ideas about what I am and what I need already. Most of our conversation revolved around the plans she had for me—exercises that are supposed to make workplace communication easier, ways to suppress my tics and twitches, that kind of thing."

Noahleen served herself another slice of pizza from the box.

"You don't sound too happy about it," she said.

"Well, I don't think I am," Clay replied. "I mean, I want to do the occupational things that will help me out at work, but I don't think that should be everything that I do. You know, I really was hoping that my therapist would be a therapist. That I could talk things over with her and that she might help me to understand some of the things that people do."

"So you want the therapist to do the thing that your wife usually does," Noahleen affected a theatrically fake Austrian accent. "Very interestink."

Clay blushed.

"Seriously, though," she went on, "if she's not helping, you need to tell her. Talk about what you expect and need. As long as you're not going to flat-out refuse to try her ideas, I'm sure she'll be negotiable. Sometimes, you just have to punch these medical types in the face a few times so that they know that you're not an ignorant patient. Let her know that you're questioning her theoretical footing and that you've read some about the other opinions out there. Even if she thoroughly debunks your ideas, you'll at least have a better understanding of the way she thinks."

"What if her problem is that she just doesn't think my diagnosis is correct?"

"Is that what you're worried about? Really?"

Clay had not thought that he was worried about this, but now that he heard himself say it, he realized that he was actually pretty terrified. Dr. Williams's demeanor, her minimization of his condition, and her focus on very surface-level physical behaviors all pointed to her not wanting to delve too deeply into his condition and his thinking process. He told Noahleen about the way she tried to add "high-functioning" to his diagnosis despite having just met him, and how she had then tried to convince him that "Asperger's" was a more fitting term. He explained why he was uncomfortable—that she had not given him any evaluations beyond an informal interview, that it was their first meeting and she had not seen enough of his behavior, and most importantly, that she was not a medical doctor.

Clay found it hard, at first, to get to the root of his thoughts. It seemed like his explanations were excuses that circled around something he did not have words for. That was exactly what he had asked Dr. Williams to work with him to improve, but even though she had said she would do that, she had spent the rest of their meeting together addressing his fidgeting and foot-tapping. When he tried to explain how he felt about this to Noahleen, though, Clay found that he just could not name the problem, even though he could see in his mind's eye exactly which of Dr. Williams's behaviors bothered him.

Noahleen, for her part, was patient. She sometimes had to ask him to repeat himself, and she also found it necessary to ask what he meant by certain words. It took time, but she unpacked everything that he was worried about. This was just what they had always done, whether or not there was a diagnosis to label the function of their communications.

In the end, Clay just pointed to what Noahleen was doing with her follow-up questions and requests for repetition and asked why it was that the therapist did nothing to poke around in his vocabulary that way.

Noahleen gave him some suggestions about how to bring this up to Dr. Williams, but Clay thought that his wife was taking it for granted that the doctor was open to being questioned. Clay was not convinced that this was the case. He was pretty sure that she was planning to give him her idea of the best treatment, and that if he did not do it, she would just claim that the reason he was not getting better was because he was not compliant. They'd seen a few dumbass neurologists do this to Noahleen when she first got sick.

He felt trapped—on the one hand, he was pretty sure that there were other therapists he could afford, but on the other hand, he could not find them without a referral, and he did not think Dr. Williams would give a 'non-compliant' patient a referral.

And what then? If he lost access to mental health resources, then who would help him document his condition to his employer? More importantly, who would help him decode the stupidly frustrating things that people demanded out of him every day?

Clay was self-aware enough to know when something was not working for him pretty quickly, but he had a hard time articulating a compromise or requesting a change. He tended to simply refuse to participate instead, and he knew that this was not an appropriate thing to do when he was going to be leading classrooms or when he was dealing with a therapist. He just did not know how to do otherwise.

Noahleen got this, but she did not have the credentials to represent him to his employer, and the person who did have those credentials— Dr. Williams—seemed to be incapable of understanding that he could not deal with her absolutes. If that was going to be the doctor's entire approach, then Clay thought he might as well be getting "therapy" from his father.

Noahleen pushed her plate away. Clay knew from experience that this meant she had made up her mind, and that what she was about to tell him was her final thought about everything that he had told her.

"It seems to me," she said, "that your biggest problem right now is that you're expecting Dr. Williams to just follow the directions the county doctors sent to her. You're expecting her to jump in and to have just absorbed all of their knowledge directly from the page, but that's not the way she's going to work. She's going to want to observe these things directly, to document them for herself. And that means that she's going to want you to jump through certain hoops until she has had enough chances to observe you."

"What if she's questioning my whole diagnosis, though? What if she wants to start at square one and treat me for something else?"

"We'll cross that bridge when we come to it. What if she sees that your diagnosis is correct, though? And what if she sees that it's not the only diagnosis, that you have some extra condition that is frustrating things and making treatment harder? I think she's right to be trying to do her own evaluation, and I would be worried if she wasn't. It's only the dumbass doctors that read a chart and then just ask you what you want to do. Just wait and see. As you said, this was just your first appointment. She doesn't really know you yet—and you don't really know her."

Clay grunted. He knew where Noahleen was going to go next. She was about to point out all the things he had done to encourage her to be compliant with her own doctors: The way that he had pushed her to stay with the tranquilizers even when they made her sleep all day, and the way that he had sided with her parents against her continuing to drive, and then later, to work.

He had been too much of a party to her own process through the medical system to kick and scream when she turned the advice back on him. He still could not shake the feeling, though, that what Dr. Williams was doing was not the same thing that Noahleen's doctors had done. He had no idea why he felt this way, but he did. Even if he pushed the feeling down and ignored it, he knew that it would come back on him.

If he suppressed it for too long, it would bubble up into an outburst, and then who knew what would happen? For now, he seemed to have no choice but to trust-fall into the situation. Either the doctor or Noahleen would eventually be able to help him. Hopefully.

❖ ❖ ❖

None Of Their Business

"Is there something you're avoiding? Something about me, or about our sessions?" Dr. Williams asked.

Clay turned his gaze from the window, where he had been watching a group of high school students play around on skateboards. It took his eyes a moment to adjust to the dim light in the room. "Why would you ask me that?"

He had not, in fact, been dwelling on any of the things that he had decided not to talk about. Now that she had accused him of holding something back though, they all flitted around in his mind, making it hard to concentrate.

"Well, it's just that we're supposed to be here to work on your social and professional communication skills, but you're spending the whole time looking out the window and answering me with grunts."

Clay grunted. Then he wished he had not, because he wanted to deny Dr. Williams's accusation.

"Look, it's not going to do us a lot of good to try to plan out a program before I know what kind of challenges you're facing. Last week, we did the basic drills that everyone does, and you seemed unhappy when you left. Instead of making me fish around with questions, why don't you tell me a little bit about what you do. Help me out. The notes I received from your last doctor said that you are a teacher."

"An instructor at the university. Down the street from here," Clay knew that these details were in the notes. He wondered if she said 'teacher' because she was generalizing or if she meant to be dismissive. "I teach a few of the basic design courses, intro to CSS & HTML, and whatever else they throw at me. It's part-time, but I usually teach twice as many classes each year as the full time faculty. Sometimes I teach more."

"I'm surprised that they allow that. It seems exploitative."

"They don't," Clay said. "I teach as much as the university will let me, and then I get the rest of my classes through one of those online schools. A different one each semester."

He outlined his work experience—the years of freelancing, his unsuccessful attempts to find a place at advertising agencies and video production companies in the area, his eventual return to graduate school, and his interest in teaching. When he reached the end of the narrative, he returned to the online schools.

"The really frustrating thing, to me, is not that online students aren't as capable or that they don't learn as well. The ones who reach out to me with questions are capable, and they do even better than most of my traditional students. The really frustrating thing is that a lot of the students online don't even try. I can tell from their site usage statistics. They just aren't logged in for long enough to really be absorbing the material. Hell, sometimes they don't even sign in for over a week, and then they act upset when they get bad grades on the major tests and projects.

"Still, I do a really good job of putting myself out there when they let me run those online classes. I don't have to talk out loud to anyone, and I can look at the message I'm about to send and revise it if need be. I also just—I have an easier time writing my thoughts out. I think I give better quality instruction that way."

"The problem is that a lot of students don't learn that way," Dr. Williams offered.

"Yeah. And those students shouldn't be in an online class. It's just not suited to their style. But they keep signing up for them. I don't know why. Maybe they just don't have a lot of self-awareness about how they learn."

They sat together in silence for a few seconds. Dr. Williams did not write anything, and she did not stare Clay down the way some other doctors would.

Finally, he spoke again. "The funny thing is, I actually get better student evaluations online than I do when I teach traditional classes. Even though more of my students are failing. Even though my regular classes have an average grade of a B-plus. For some reason, the students who never meet me think that I'm really good at this, even when they don't do the work they're supposed to do. The ones that really learn the material, the ones in face to face classes I mean, they are more critical. They never point out what they want to change, though. They just give me lower scores, and they don't say anything about why."

"Do you think that it's something that you do, or do you think that's just the difference between the two class formats?"

Clay fidgeted. When he spoke, he surprised himself with the petulance in his own voice.

"You tell me. Ever since I was a really little kid, I've had this sense that everyone is always secretly laughing at me. I've never been able to tell the difference between someone who really cares about what I'm talking about and someone who's just waiting for me to go away. It's caused some problems."

"So you think that part of the problem is that you might not be engaging students. And, on top of that, you're worried that you are not able to tell when that's happening, so you don't shift topics when you lose them?"

Clay nodded.

"That sounds like the kind of thing that they build on in professional development."

"They do, but their ideas don't always work. And there's not a lot of professional development and pedagogy happening within my department itself. I'm stuck using the general suggestions that the university puts out as across-the-curriculum events. I don't know why that is. Maybe there's just not a lot of pedagogy about graphic design in general?"

Dr. Williams wrote for a moment. "Are you afraid that you're going to lose your job?"

"To be honest, yes. I'm always afraid of that. Or, at least, I'm often afraid of that. It's getting better now, because the university has new rules in place about seniority and guaranteed return. Before that, I was constantly in fear of just not being offered classes, either because the enrollment had shifted or because someone I didn't know was lobbying to get a few classes thrown to a friend, or whatever. Now, that's not so big a concern. Since I can't really tell whether the full-time people like me or not, having that policy that says I have to actually get written up for misconduct before they'll give me the boot is really nice."

"No," Dr. Williams dropped her pen into her notebook and closed it. "I mean, do you worry that any of these issues with your students are going to get you fired?"

It took Clay a minute to process what she was asking. It made no sense. He was doing everything he could to improve, and he was responsive to questions, putting in the hours—why would he worry about getting fired? Who fired people for being concerned about their own improvement?

He reeled in his frustration, but he could tell it was affecting the way he talked when he said, "No. I have above average evaluations, even at my worst. I just want to do as good a job in-seat as I do online, and I want to keep getting better at both. I know I'm doing what the university wants me to do. My observation notes, when they come and watch my class, only ever show me minor bits of advice.

"I want to get a better handle on why I can't tell the difference between my best and my worst lessons. And I want to figure out how to talk to the students who don't get me. That's what this is all about, right? Working on my awareness and my ability to fit in? If I can't tell why students are frustrated, why they keep asking me the same questions over and over again after I've just answered them in the lecture, and why they never seem to remember what the textbook said, how am I supposed to give them the best performance I can give?"

He realized, after he finished, that his volume had gotten out of control.

"I'm sorry I shouted," he said. "That happens sometimes when I talk for too long."

"I'll admit that it surprised me how upset you became," Dr. Williams said.

"I'm not upset, I just... I didn't realize that what you were hearing wasn't what I thought I was saying."

"I think I see," she said. "What's the end goal here, for you? Assume we can get your evaluations up, where does that lead you? To a full-time job? Back into the industry, to work for an advertising firm? What do you want out of this situation?"

"Well," Clay said, "I have to be honest. I can't really think further into the future than just making enough money to be able to get myself health insurance again. I haven't had any for a bit, and now I'm working too much to get Medicaid. I'm in a situation where if I got hurt or sick or something, I'd have to quit coming to therapy to be able to afford my medication."

Dr. Williams opened her book again and started scribbling. "Okay. But really, if that was solved, what would you want?"

Clay shrugged. He wished he could answer the question. Briefly, he thought about being fifteen again and looking good in a leather skirt, but he knew that there was nothing Dr. Williams could do to fulfill that want. He also thought about the good years in his past, about building up his freelance business while Noahleen worked. He thought about the triumph he felt when he had earned enough to finance the down payment on their house, and the disappointment that he felt when they were forced to sell the house to pay for her medical expenses.

The truth was, he just felt so far behind that he could not really articulate any goals beyond catching up. When he finally spoke, he tried to make sure that his words reflected that without lecturing the doctor too much.

"I guess I just want to feel like I'm not disabled," he said. "I know you can't cure me, but I'd like to be able to function in a way where my disability doesn't impact the quality of my work."

"Okay," Dr. Williams said. "So what I'm hearing is that you don't really feel like its any of your employer's business whether you're autistic or not. I take it then, that you haven't told them?"

Clay shook his head. He hated the way Dr. Williams put words in his mouth, but he did not have the words to tell her why she should stop.

"I thought about disclosing at work, but I wanted to know what I should say. I know they're supposed to work with me, and they can't fire me for my disability, but I've been afraid that they might find a different excuse to fire me once they knew about it. I was kind of hoping that you would tell me what to ask them for."

Dr. Williams nodded. She finished writing whatever it was she wrote in her notebooks while he talked. Then, for the first time since the session started, she looked him in the eye.

"Don't tell them anything," she said. "It's none of their business. We're going to handle it ourselves, you and me."

The Routine

"Remember what we talked about before the semester started. You want to take a breath and a half after you hear a question before you rattle off the answer. A breath and a half. Otherwise, you seem impatient, and it seems condescending. Students will think they should have known the answer and that they asked a stupid question."

Noahleen's hands were busy with the iron. She talked while she watched the shirt, making sure that she worked from one end to the other so that she would not iron herself into a corner.

Clay sipped coffee in his slacks and undershirt, taking notes on an index card as she talked.

"What if it is a stupid question?" he asked.

"Pretend it's not," she replied. "I know how some professors get, but you're not tenured and you're not seventy years old, so no one's going to shrug it off if you make the students feel like you're only there to punish them when they step out of line. Your goal is to drag them across the finish line, to make the material accessible, and to leave as few behind as possible."

"I know that, but sometimes they don't follow directions. It's annoying."

"Pretend it's not," she said again.

Clay grunted. Noahleen said nothing in reply. When he finished jotting down her notes on his index card, he flipped it over and doodled diagrams on the back. They were loose but functional flow charts showing the relationship between the last few weeks' lessons and the one he had planned for that day.

"We're floating divs now," he said. "That can be pretty tricky, but if they got last week's lesson, then it shouldn't be anything that they can't get right with a little trial and error."

He gave her a long moment to reply, and when she stayed silent, Clay turned to look at his wife.

She seemed to be done ironing the shirt, but she had not taken it off the ironing board. Instead, she stared out the window, iron in hand, as if she had been turned off mid-chore.

"Hey," he called, "are you okay?"

When she said nothing, he clapped his hands together. She startled then and looked at him. The iron came down on his shirt. It rested there without moving. Steam billowed around it.

Clay crossed from the kitchen to the living room in three large steps. Before he even thought about what he was doing, he had the iron in one hand and his shirt in the other. Noahleen stared up at him, her eyes as wide as if he had just shouted at her.

"What? I'm ironing."

"Are you sure? You're okay?" he set the iron down and turned it off.

Noahleen grimaced at him. "What the hell is wrong with you? Of course I'm okay. Why are you just snatching things out of my hands?"

Clay took a step backward and then slipped his shirt on, buttoning it up as he talked.

"I'm sorry. You just stopped. You weren't answering me, and you were holding the iron up in the air like you were paused mid-motion. I thought maybe you were having a seizure."

At the word 'seizure,' Noahleen's hands went to her hips and she scowled.

"I did not have a seizure."

"Okay," Clay said. "You didn't have a seizure. You'd know it if you did. But can you blame me for being worried?"

"I was just looking out the window."

He tucked his shirt in. "Fine. You were looking out the window. But you weren't responding to me anymore, and you didn't set the iron aside, and then you just left it on my shirt."

"I was just distracted, okay? It's not a seizure."

Clay put his hands up. "I surrender, okay? I just wanted to make sure, because that kind of thing worries me."

"I don't have seizures that look like that."

"Well, sometimes you do. You don't remember them because you black out."

She cocked her head at him.

"Just trust me. You do. This one wasn't a seizure, okay? I'm not arguing about that. But sometimes, you have seizures just like that, so I can't always tell."

Clay went back into the kitchen and sipped at his coffee. The clock on the oven said nine-thirty exactly. He would have to be out the door in ten minutes. He glanced at the kitchen table and saw that his laptop was already packed up. The index card was full. He had ten minutes to enjoy the coffee before he had to leave.

Noahleen followed him into the kitchen and stood too close.

"It wasn't a seizure."

"Do you see me calling in to work so that I can stay with you? I believe you, it wasn't a seizure."

"You don't sound like you believe me."

"I'm going to work, aren't I?"

"No. You're sipping your coffee."

Clay rolled his eyes. It was a bad habit, and if Noahleen had him doing it, then there was little to no chance he would be able to avoid it once his students' questions started. Inside himself, he felt something clench.

"I don't have time for this," he said, "and I can't afford to have it hanging over my head when I walk into the classroom. What's the problem?"

Noahleen backed away. "Nothing."

"Come on, Noahleen. I know it isn't nothing. First you were staring off into space like your brain evaporated, and then you started picking a fight. Just tell me what's going on so that I can help you with it, and then I can go to work."

She retreated into the living room and collapsed the ironing board so that she could put it away.

"No, you're right. You don't have time. Just finish your coffee and go to work."

Clay's confusion started to burn. He tried to ignore it, but that just turned it into anger.

"For fuck's sake, Noahleen, you know I'm not going to stop dwelling on it all day, so just spit it out. Whatever it is isn't going to be as bad as my obsessing over the mystery when I'm supposed to be concentrating on my job."

She leaned the ironing board against the couch and turned on him.

"Fine. You want to know what's wrong? I feel like a freeloading asshole, that's what's wrong."

Clay flinched. He had not been expecting the heat her voice carried.

"I've been stuck doing nothing for years, and now you're starting to get really good at what you do, and your therapy is going to make it even easier for you to get ahead, and... and I just want to contribute something."

Clay followed her into the living room and put his arms around her.

"You are contributing," he said. "Do you think I'd be doing this well if you didn't take the time to review my approach with my students? Do you think that my performance reviews would still be climbing if you didn't go over the lessons with me and point out the confusing parts? I need you to show me when the kids won't understand what I'm saying. You ground me."

"I know," she said. She leaned into his hug, but she did not return it. "I just miss being able to get in the car and go someplace else. I don't like asking you to take me out when you get home because you're always so tired, but I might go crazy if I dont leave the house more. And I'd rather leave it to accomplish something and not just to go out and spend money."

Clay stepped back so that he could look down at her face. It was awkward, but their height difference made it necessary.

"I'm not going to tell you what to do," he said. "But there is a bus stop at the end of the block, and there are things you can do— volunteer things, or arts and crafts, or whatever. Learn the bus schedule and go exploring. You haven't had a serious episode in months. Just bring your emergency medication and go exploring."

"I don't know."

He let her go completely and walked to the kitchen table. As he lifted his bag, he looked back at her.

"If you don't want to take the bus, then find something you can go do in the evening. I'll drop you off, and then I'll go sit in a coffee shop and do my grading or something. I'll make sure you get out to do things. Just figure out what you want."

Noahleen nodded.

Clay slipped out the door and into the garage. He hoped that she would get lucky and find something that interested her quickly. He hated to see her hurt, but he had no idea how to solve this problem.

Losing Control

Clay sat in his office and stared at the wall. His mistake kept playing in his head. Again and again, he reviewed what had happened, trying to find the place where he might have done things differently and avoided the train wreck that the day had become. Each time, he wound up in the same place—humiliated, confused, and stuck in the classroom for forty minutes of useless, sidetracked time that he could not end without getting himself into trouble.

He did not blame Noahleen, but he was keenly aware that he had let her problems this morning unsettle him. He had remained unsettled through the entire drive to the university, despite his best attempts to reset his focus by turning up the stereo and letting The Prodigy infuse him with focus and momentum. It had helped, but not enough. Walking from the parking garage to the class building had still been a nightmare.

His sunglasses were not strong enough to keep the morning light from reaching into the back of his eyes and stirring up a headache. Down his back, Clay felt the sticky beginnings of sweat causing his underclothes to bunch and pull.

That had been the beginning of the problem. It was one thing for him to be distracted or a little upset in class, that just happened. When his clothes constricted around him like a mobile prison, though, it became impossible for Clay to hold his temper. Most of the time when that happened, he excused himself to a private restroom or locked his office door and undressed. A few minutes without the clothes, together with the un-bunching and rearranging of them as he re-dressed, usually reset his mood.

He had not been able to do that today, though. Today, he had been running late. Too late to stop in the bathroom for fifteen minutes without keeping the class waiting. As he reviewed his behavior over and over, it became harder and harder to keep himself from believing it was Noahleen's fault.

This conclusion made him feel guilty, because he knew intellectually that his behavior was not her fault, but his emotions kept betraying him. It also made him frustrated, because they were *his* emotions and he should be able to control them. That guilt pulled him further into himself, compelling him to go over the events of the morning again, to argue against his own feelings.

In class, he had stuttered through his presentation. Hearing himself stutter made him nervous, which just made him stutter more. He hated that something he usually enjoyed—something he usually coasted through—was such a challenge. At one point, he accidentally skipped over a definition for a term, and a lone hand at the back of the room shot up. He took the question and backtracked, but he felt himself getting hot around the collar.

Not long after that, he heard the giggles. He could tell that they were objectively quiet, but nothing was quiet to Clay just then. The stifled mockery that was always present somewhere in the classroom, whether in large or small amounts, started to eat away at him. As it did, he stumbled more and became more aware of the giggling. If only he could figure out where it was coming from. The room was dark, though, and the light from the projector blinded him to his audience. He usually preferred it that way. He used it—the bright, hot light— like armor against his anxiety. Today, though, it turned against him, putting him more clearly in the spotlight and pinning him to the stage.

Having lost his place, he started over at the beginning of the section. He heard the students groan as he did it. Checking his watch, he saw that he was running into the portion of the class that was usually set aside for the computer lab. No wonder they were getting fidgety.

"Look," he said, "I know we usually go to the lab to futz with the new commands a bit, but we might not make it there today."

A collective groan worked its way through the room, fracturing his class into pockets of more or less disappointed students. A second later, he heard the sounds of several books closing while backpacks thumped onto tables.

"We're not done here," Clay said.

"Sure we are," said the voice from the back that had asked the question earlier. "This shit is simple, and we're not going to sit through another review of it when we could get in the lab and get our hands dirty."

Clay opened his mouth to reply, but just at that moment the door at the back of the room opened, creating a new square of bright light that competed against the spotlights above Clay's head. As he squinted against it, he saw no less than ten bodies in silhouette, all fleeing his classroom.

That was when he gave up.

"Turn the lights back on," he said.

No one did.

"Can someone get to the back and flip the lights on?" he asked.

Several seconds later, the fluorescents in the ceiling flickered and spat, and then the room was visible to him again. With the exception of the one girl standing next to the light switch, the back row of the classroom was empty.

"Are you going to finish the lecture?"

Clay had no idea who said it, but he knew it was from the front row.

"No. The lecture's done."

He was still staring at the girl by the lightswitch. The scuffling and bumping sounds of students dismissing themselves filled the room.

"I didn't say class was over!"

He had not meant to shout it. Still, the entire room froze because he did. The lightswitch girl cringed. He was staring at her when he yelled.

Clay looked down at the desk. He needed a piece of paper. Any piece of paper would do.

There was a flier for an international student dinner. He flipped it over. The back was clean.

"I'm sending around an attendance sheet," he said. "I want to know who left. Then we're going to the computer lab."

Another groan. He handed someone the flier and a pen.

"It's no use bitching about it. Class is still in session. At least you're getting credit for the activity that we're going to do."

Lightswitch girl put her hand up. She was still in the back of the room.

"Yes?" Clay asked.

"Some of us needed that lecture. Will you help us with the activity if we get stuck?"

"No," Clay said. His temples throbbed and then, suddenly, his feet hurt. "It's a pop quiz. Open book, but you only have until the end of class to finish. No help. You should have been doing the reading."

"But—"

"No buts," he said. "I tried to give the lecture. Thank your classmates for leaving if you feel badly about it."

"That's not fair!" a new voice said. This one was closer to the front. He intentionally did not look for who it was. "You're already punishing the people who left by giving graded work. Why are you going to punish the people who wanted to stay and learn?"

Clay bristled. He felt his eyes start to roll and tried to stop them. He had no idea whether he was successful or not.

"I'm not punishing anyone," he snapped. "If you can't understand what's in the book, you're not working hard enough. This is a college class."

He heard the protester get up and collect her books. A few seconds later, when she crossed into his field of vision, he noticed that it was one of his A students. He winced. This was getting out of hand.

She walked out without causing a fuss.

"Anyone else?" he asked. He was hoping the rest of them would just walk out, too. Then he could go back to his office without getting in trouble for cancelling class.

When no one else moved, he unplugged his laptop from the projector and grabbed his bag.

"Let's go to the lab then," he said.

Later, in his office, it was easy to see how everything had fallen apart. In the moment, though, all he knew was that the contract that usually held his students in his orbit had fallen apart. He was forced by this fact to ad-lib against his own nature, because the ones who had abandoned the process deserved to be punished.

Clay wanted to help out the remaining members of the class, but it was all he could do to keep himself from running away and tearing his clothes off so that he could breathe freely. Under no circumstances did he want to keep talking to strange teenagers. Sooner or later, they would need to do for themselves anyway.

A few minutes later, in the computer lab, he had to force his voice to remain even.

"Contrary to what some people think," he said, "a pop quiz is not a punishment. Hell, it's not even high-stakes. I'm looking for you to use a floating div to properly organize photos and captions without having to resort to a table. You can use whatever assets you were already working with, but you have to create a page of photos and captions—a gallery, or else a directory of employees, award recipients... you get the idea. Show me that you can size them and float them in relationship to each other. That's the whole quiz."

A hand shot up. It was just too much to think about.

"I'm not taking questions until after class. You have your assignment."

Finally, he had the chance to sit down. He opened his laptop so that the class would think he was grading or doing something, but then he let his eyes unfocus. One by one, his students emailed him the links to their documents. He opened each one and, without comment, added them into the gradebook.

After half the class had finished, he realized that no one was leaving when they were done.

"You can go if you have nothing else to work on," he said.

A hand shot up again. One of the few boys left in the group.

"Yes?"

"Will you be giving us comments to let us know what we did right or wrong?"

"Not this time," Clay said. "From what I'm seeing, everyone has the basics down. Think of it this way—this quiz is less about whether you're doing it right and more about letting me know if there's something a large portion of the class is doing wrong. If that happens, then we'll review the lesson. Otherwise, you'll be fine if we just move forward."

The student nodded and then stared down at his screen.

Clay had felt like he should say something else, but he did not know what. In his office, reflecting on the event, he waited for it to come to him. Instead, his imagination called up that earlier confrontation with Noahleen and played it for him again.

Clay hoped that the next class would be better. It was a second-level group doing computer lab time, so at least he would not need to worry about speaking.

Usually, his office time was when he did his grading. Today, though, it was an endless hell of reviewing the class over and over again. Despite his best attempts to do his work, Clay's memory kept forcing him back into the classroom, showing him where his careful control snapped and curled back against itself. Even reading the news did not help.

He hated feeling this way, but his hatred did not bring him any further insight. Instead, it just redirected his attention back to the events of the day. Again.

❖ ❖ ❖

Communication Gap

Clay gulped down the scent of Noahleen's hair. His hands slipped down from her shoulders to the small of her back. She squeezed him, but otherwise she did not move.

"I love you *so* much," she said. "You look like you've had a bad day."

He mumbled something into her hair. Neither of them knew what it was. His hands rubbed the spot right over her spine, where the hollow of her lower back was deepest. Noahleen's knees sagged, but then she unwrapped herself from their embrace and pushed him away.

"Not now," she said. "Are you hungry?"

Clay shook his head. Words were not going to be his friend tonight. He touched her waist, but he made sure not to grab at it. He needed her wrapped around him. He needed the pressure of her body to keep himself from floating away. He thought about how he used to hide in closets and under beds, packing himself tightly into spaces so that he could feel the weight of other things on his body. More than fucking, he needed her to hold him down, to compress him until the pockets of empty inside his chest disappeared and he forgot the problems of the day.

She pulled away from him, though, leaving fifteen inches of aching emptiness between them. Just enough that he could not reach down to her waist. Just enough that he could only lightly stroke her arm around the elbow. Not enough to be running away, but enough to tell him "no."

He stepped back. If they were going to be apart, then Clay needed her outside of his space.

"Are you hungry?" This time when she said it, it was clear that she really meant "I am hungry."

"I'm not, but I could cook," he said. "Maybe the smells will jog my appetite."

"Never mind," she said. She walked away from him and into the bedroom, shutting the door behind herself.

Clay wanted to follow her, but instead he sat on the couch. Whatever led her to retreat, she would eventually let him know. He thought about starting dinner so that he could surprise her, but he worried about choosing the right meal. If he chose wrong, it might complicate whatever was filling the distance between their bodies. It was better to just wait until she made it clear what she wanted.

The TV stared at him with its big empty face that looked like a shadowy reflection of his own face. It was begging him to switch it on. He thought about it, but decided the noise would just make him feel worse. There were only judge shows and reruns of sitcoms from the 1990s to choose from at this time of day anyway.

So Clay sat. For how long, he could not be sure. He intentionally avoided looking at the clock. Once, he heard Noahleen pass from the bedroom to the bathroom and back, but he did not acknowledge her. If she wanted him nearby, she could make the first move.

His resolve faltered before hers did. He felt himself getting hungry, and the hunger reminded him that he had other work to do before he could really rest. He would have to nudge whatever this tension was toward a resolution.

Clay heaved his bulk off the couch and walked to the bedroom, to Noahleen. She sat in the center of the bed, holding her head in her hands and letting all of her dark hair cover her body like a curtain. Clay sat on the bed, but he kept his distance and his silence.

"I'm sorry," Noahleen said.

"Sorry about what?" Clay found himself confused.

"I'm sorry about this morning. And I'm sorry that I'm still upset about this morning. I'm sorry about shaking you up right before you left, and I'm sorry that I'm not happy, and I'm sorry that I'm not being more available to you so that you can talk about what's happening with work and therapy and everything."

"I don't feel like you're unavailable. And I don't expect you to just sit there and mind me while I try to deal with work and everything. What do you think we have going on here?"

She shook her head. "I just feel like, you know, I'm not working so I should take care of the house. Like I'm doing something wrong if I just sit around and wait for you to come home from work. Especially if you're going to just go to town on the housework when you get home. If I'm not keeping this place up and I'm not making a contribution to our income, what am I? What good is it for you to stick with me any more? I'm just draining your resources."

It took a few seconds for Clay to consider Noahleen's words. It was difficult for him to do so, because he wanted to just reject everything she said as a lie. He knew, though, that accusing her of lying would just lead to them fighting. Even so, it was hard for him to make his brain engage with statements that just *were not so*, and comforting nothings took forever for him to produce.

Meanwhile, she sobbed.

"Why don't you think you're contributing?" he finally asked. "You're recovering. You're doing more every day, and we're slowly but surely getting to an equilibrium. You had a section of your brain removed from your head a couple of years ago. You're on four different tranquilizers. It's not surprising that you can't work or that you might get tired from doing basic chores. Why should you feel bad about it? You did the physical therapy, the rest is just letting yourself work up some endurance."

He rubbed her back.

"Besides, I never expected or asked you to do all the housework. How could I hold it against you if I never even talked about it with you?"

"I know," she said. "You think I don't know? Nothing I'm feeling makes sense, and that makes it worse, because I'm wasting your time and I'm upsetting you, and there isn't even a good reason for it. I really wish I could just stop, but I can't. I need to do something."

"Have you thought about going back to work? Just, you know, part-time. Just a little so that you can start getting back into the swing of things, to see whether or not you still want to do the same thing."

She shook her head. Her hands were still planted firmly on her face.

"I just can't. If they saw the way I am now—the way I walk, and the way my left hand has gotten clumsy since the surgery... I can't go back. And I'm pretty sure that a company that doesn't know me yet wouldn't hire me. Who wants a part-time worker who can't hold a schedule and can't meet with clients because she's too spaced out on tranquilizers? I'm too embarrassed to even ask. I don't want them to see me this way."

Clay pulled away from her. He wanted to say something kind, but the way she talked about herself upset him. If it had been anyone but her saying these things about her, he would have started a fight with them by now. He swallowed his bile and focused his attention on making her feel better instead of being more right than her.

"So you need something new to do."

Noahleen finally dropped her hands from her face. "You're fucking brilliant. Why didn't I think of that?"

"No, I mean... I mean that I tried to start a business while you worked." Clay was having a hard time speaking because Noahleen was giving him a dead-eyed stare. "Maybe you could do it this time. Maybe there's something you could do at home, for yourself. That way, you don't have to work on someone else's schedule. You don't have to try to support the whole house. You can contribute on your good days, and you can work on your recovery on the ungood days."

"Yeah, but what?" she asked. "It's all well and good that you can just proclaim 'start a business,' but I don't have any idea what I could even do."

He shrugged. "I don't know. If you feel like you need to contribute, though, maybe you could start by figuring out which parts of the housework you want to do, and then you can spend the rest of your time exploring options for working from home. And whatever you decide you hate doing for housework, I'll keep doing. I did all of it back when you were working. I know how."

She shrugged. He tried to hold her again, but she still pulled away and told him once more that she was not in the mood. Then she got up and went into the kitchen to put dinner together, leaving Clay on the bed, wondering why it was that she seemed to always think that his touching her was a prelude to sex.

❖ ❖ ❖

Shutdown

"Do you understand now how important it is to avoid talking about your mental health situation while you are at work?" Dr. Williams's eyes narrowed at Clay. "Do you see how much worse it could have been?"

Clay shrugged. He had felt like cancelling his appointment today, but Noahleen convinced him that the days he needed to go to therapy most were the days that he wanted to cancel. Still, it was hard to focus on Dr. Williams with all the memories shouting at him right now— memories of his classroom management problems and the instability Noahleen's seizures caused.

"Clay, you need to pay attention to this. It's important." Dr. Williams pointed her pen at him. "If your students are already pushing back against your leadership, then you don't want to hand them any excuses they can use to rationalize their misbehavior. I know you're thinking that you can just disclose through Human Resources or just ask your boss for help or something. Everyone thinks that. Consider, though, the way that individuals work. You're right that the disclosure would protect you from official retaliation. But would it protect you?"

Clay focused his eyes on a dark spot on the wall. He wondered if Dr. Williams had smashed a bug there or if it was just a trick of light and shadow. He wanted to interrupt her and tell her that he had no intention of using autism as a defense against the student complaints he had gotten during the last week, but he knew that she would just scold him for interrupting and then finish her lecture anyway. She had been doing that a lot during their last couple of sessions.

"Do you even listen while we're in these sessions? Or are you just putting in time?"

Clay looked away from the spot on the wall and into Dr. Williams's eyes. He knew he would not be able to keep it up for very long, so he did not try to talk until he looked away from her again.

"I'm listening," he said. "But I'm not hearing anything. You want to lecture me about why I should listen to your recommendations while I'm already following them. That's fine. Since you're just telling me to do what I already do, I expect that this isn't part of our hour yet. If it is, then I'd like to talk about the things that I need to talk about."

Dr. Williams opened her mouth to speak, but then she sat back in her chair and blew air out through her lips instead. "Okay. You're right. You are following my advice, you haven't disclosed at work, and you didn't even mention wanting to. Fine. That topic's put to bed. What's bothering you this week, Clay?"

He crossed and uncrossed his legs.

"Well, like I told you just a few minutes ago, I've had some student complaints this week. Dr. Kalkaska was pretty supportive, but still, they happened. She mostly told the complaining students that they need to stay in class and that there's no recourse for them if they walk out on a lecture and wind up missing work, whether they knew they'd be missing it or not. The thing that bothered me, though, was that she told me that I need to be less condescending, and I don't see how I was being condescending. She said I'd been rolling my eyes at the students, but I don't think I did that. I mean, I know I do that sometimes, but I am pretty sure I didn't do it then. How can I tell?"

Dr. Williams shrugged. "I don't know what you want me to say. I wasn't there to see it. I can see where someone would think you're condescending sometimes, though. Did you want to work on that?"

Clay nodded.

"Okay, so here's what you do—"

"Wait." He put his hands up. "What do I do that makes me seem condescending?"

"I don't know what you mean."

"Well, you're about to tell me what to do to seem less condescending. That's good, but how do I know when I need to do it? What should I look out for as a sign that I'm about to get condescending toward someone? I don't have any idea why people accuse me of acting this way. What good is it going to do to teach me how to act differently if I don't know when to start using your tips?"

Dr. Williams's lips tightened. "Just do this all the time."

"But—"

"Do me a favor? Hear what I have to say before you interrupt me again."

"Fine."

Clay did not hear Dr. Williams, though. He tried to listen to her, but the sound of his blood thrumming in his ears drowned her out. He took deeper breaths, hoping to calm himself enough to be able to hear what she was trying to say, but his heart beat harder and faster, making the sound in his ears even worse. He told himself that she was doing the best that she could, that he needed to find a way to make himself clearer to her, and that he should be listening because what she was saying might be a simple social protocol that he could always follow, like smiling during a greeting or shaking hands.

It really did not matter what he told himself. All he heard was blood rushing in his ears. It was just like when he was a child and his father scolded him for something that he did not believe it was wrong to do, like bouncing his legs during church. No matter how much he wanted to be part of what was happening, keeping himself in check pulled his world inward and made it impossible for him to focus on anything other than his own body.

He nodded along, though, so that he would not be accused of being rude. He had learned to do that a long time ago.

Without Dr. Williams's voice distracting him, he considered whether or not he actually wanted to tell Dr. Kalkaska about his condition. He had worked with her for five years, after all. Not just as an instructor, either. She had taught many of the graduate-level seminars when he was going after his master's degree. His relationship with her was almost as long as any in his professional life, and he was pretty sure that she would make sure he was all right.

"Are you all right?"

Clay ignored the voice at first. It was not uncommon for him to hear other people talking to him when he thought about them. When the question was repeated, though, he nodded.

When he heard "Are you all right?" for the third time, he looked around, and only then did he notice that it was not Imaginary-Dr.-Kalkaska's voice he was hearing, it was Dr. Williams's. She was out of her seat and waving her arms in front of his face. Her words seemed not to line up with the movements her lips were making.

"I'm okay," he said. "You can stop waving."

He stood up to show her that he was fine. As soon as he did, the room tilted sideways and the floor ran straight at the side of his head. Clay did not even have enough time to try to catch himself before hitting the ground. Struggling to comprehend what was happening, he opened his mouth to ask questions, but something filled his throat, making him gag. It was all he could do to cough through it so that he could breathe.

Hands touched him, opening his shirt. He felt embarrassed and tried to stop them. They grew more insistent. He thought about punching, but then it occurred to him that the hands probably belonged to Dr. Williams. He forced his hands to be still so that he would not hurt her accidentally, but he still tried to shake his head no.

Dr. Williams must not have noticed his head shaking, because her hands roamed over him, probing. He felt his clothing loosen. He felt cold air against his feet. Where were his shoes?

Why would she take off his shoes?

The world came into sharp focus. It was a bracing sensation, like landing face first in the snow. He saw Dr. Williams leaning over him then, her arms extended. He felt her hands on his chest. It suddenly occurred to him that she was trying to start CPR.

He still wondered why she had taken off his shoes first.

Clay started to feel hot in his face and hands. All he wanted to do was run away from Dr. Williams and never come back. It was just too embarrassing to think about coming back. He pushed her away and sat up.

"Are you okay?" she asked again.

"I think so," he said.

"I think you might want to go to the emergency room and get checked out. I think you just had a panic attack, but it could be something more serious."

Clay shook his head. "I can't do that. I don't have any insurance. I can barely afford this." He gestured at the office around them.

He tried to stand, but Dr. Williams pushed him back down.

"At least sit still." She sighed. "Therapy won't do you much good if you die of a heart attack."

"I don't make the rules I live by," he said. "I'm doing what I can afford to do to stay healthy."

She pursed her lips and made a noise. Then she stood up.

"Does this happen very often?"

He thought about the way his clothes bunched and pulled at him whenever he got upset. "Kind of. Not this bad. It only gets this bad sometimes."

Suddenly Dr. Williams was all business again. The concern he had seen in her face when she was getting ready to perform CPR folded itself back up into her features and went away. She was a psychologist again.

"Let's talk about how this impacts your teaching. Did you have one of these attacks on the day that you had problems with classroom discipline? Were you trying to teach in this condition when the student complained about you?"

Clay took a deep breath, and then he did his best to answer all of Dr. Williams's questions. They were invasive, but at least she was finally asking him about something important.

❖ ❖ ❖

Meltdown

Grading, at least, was easy for Clay to do. It never mattered whether he was having a good day or not, evaluating student work was a reflex: he did it quickly, without thinking, and with a consistency that was often unnerving to observers. Anyone watching him work would assume that he was having an extraordinarily productive day. In reality his mind was spinning, and he could not concentrate. Halfway through scoring the essay questions on a unit test for his Honors group, he suddenly realized that he could not remember any of the answers from the first dozen students.

Checking his marks, he found no mistakes, but he still felt anxious about having allowed himself to zombie grade. If anyone ever discovered that he was prone to these inattentive fits...

Clay began to see why Dr. Williams did not want him to disclose his condition. His entitlement to "reasonable" accommodations under the law might protect him in a lot of ways, but it might also lead to rulings against him or to people assuming that his anxiety and staring spells were proof that he was not diligent enough to lead a classroom. As Clay understood it, the law did allow that barriers might put certain things out of the reach of "reasonable" accommodation. What if Clay's problems were judged to be on the wrong side of those barriers? What would happen to him then?

His eyes itched. Was it from stress or from staring too long at sloppy handwriting? Did it matter? He wanted a break. He needed a break. He just could not afford to give himself a break. Dealing with the extra meetings and paperwork that came with the student complaints he had received a couple of weeks ago had eaten up his on-campus time. Insomnia and Noahleen's problems had taken a lot of his time at home. At this point, if he took a break, he would not finish the grading.

Still, his eyes itched.

Clay immersed himself in his process. After a few more tests, he backtracked again and re-read because he was just not absorbing or remembering anything.

"Clay? Are you in there?" The door muffled Noahleen's voice.

"Yeah. I'm here."

The door opened, and she stepped into the room. When she saw the pile of tests out on the desk, she backpedaled a half step.

"I'm sorry," she said. "I'll just wait until you're done."

"No." He closed his eyes and massaged the bridge of his nose. "I'm not getting anywhere. Just tell me what you want."

"It's okay," she said. "It's not important."

She reached for the doorknob.

Frustration surged in Clay's head, making it feel heavy—too heavy for his neck to support. As it tilted forward, he felt the muscles on either side of his neck bunch up, and the resulting cramp was far worse than the itching in his eyes had been.

"Just fucking spit it out!" he shouted.

Noahleen recoiled.

"Sorry," Clay said, "I'm just… Sorry. Just tell me what you wanted."

"Are you okay?"

This was getting out of hand. All he wanted to do was finish his grading, so that he could regain some sense of control over his daily tasks. He knew that Noahleen did not really want to be an obstacle to that, but still, he could not stop himself from lashing out at her. Experience told him that this would force him to spend the rest of the day talking through this fight, but he was powerless to stop himself. It was like he was in a building, staring out the window at an intersection where a car crash was just a few seconds away from happening.

"I'm fine! Just get to the point!"

The words echoed in his ears. In his mind's eye he watched all the other times that this exact fight had happened over the last decade. It seemed like it was more common, now that Noahleen could not work. He wondered if his memory was correct about that or if he was just romanticizing their life before the seizures and the brain surgery.

Noahleen put her hands on her hips, and Clay began to understand that they would be fighting for a good long time.

"I had an idea about what I could do to make some money, and I wanted you to tell me if we have the budget and if it sounds like a good idea. This might not be the time, that's okay, but you don't have to be a dick about it! You're the one who told me to figure out how to start a business, and you told me to come in. Don't yell at me like I'm forcing myself on you."

Clay willed himself to apologize with every ounce of his being, but instead his muscles snapped taut and his fingers and toes twisted against the sensation. The cramp in his neck spread through his entire body, and he clutched the edge of his desk waiting for it to pass. It escalated instead. He stopped breathing.

When he opened his mouth to say something, Clay found himself screaming. At first, there were no words, but then he heard himself telling Noahleen that if she would have just walked in and asked the question she wanted to ask, that he would already be back to grading papers. He hated himself for blaming her, because he knew that she could not help being indirect sometimes, it was just who she was.

Finally, he lost his words and his voice, and his criticisms trailed off into deep panting. Noahleen ran away from him and into their bedroom. The lock on the door clicked.

Clay's chest collapsed, and all of the energy and tension that had been running through him drained into his core and flushed itself into a sinking emptiness in his midsection. He staggered and had to steady himself on his desktop. His fingers brushed the keyboard when he did, and it skittered away as if someone had bumped into it forcefully. It was amusing how light the keyboard had become, and then he panicked for a second when he brushed against the monitor and it teetered, almost falling off the desk. After he reached out to steady it, it completed its fall.

Drifting lazily through the doorway and into the hall, Clay felt like a balloon. He came to rest against the bedroom door frame.

Why was he so exhausted and confused? Just moments ago he had been wide awake.

"Honey?" he said to the door.

There was no response from the other side. Maybe he had only imagined he was speaking. Maybe he had just mouthed the words, forgetting to put the breath into them that gave them sound.

He tried again.

"Honey?"

That attempt had some teeth to it. There was movement on the other side of the door, but after a few seconds it stopped.

Clay imagined himself pounding on the door and pleading for Noahleen to open it so he could apologize. It seemed like a very bad idea. If he did such a thing, then Noahleen would only tell him what he wanted to hear. Afterward, she would hate him for demanding her attention, for forcing her to put her anger aside before she was ready. This was somehow very clear to him, even though it was not the kind of thing he normally thought about at all.

Not wanting to be a bully, he stepped away from the door. The air in the apartment was stagnant and too hot. Clay was weak, and this weakness was what had turned him into a balloon. He let himself glide toward the front door. Once the doorknob was within reach, he pulled at it frantically. There was healthier air on the other side, air that would not choke him and press him too closely.

In an instant he was through the door, and the outside was cooler. The concrete around him in the open-air stairwell was draining the heat away from him, shrinking him, giving him weight.

Why did everything hurt so much?

Just as soon as he grasped onto that thought, the sun cut through the clouds and lit everything up, piercing his eyes and forcing him to turn back toward the building. Hiding from the sun made Clay feel like a vampire.

Was he a vampire? Had he just been a parasite all these years, attached to Noahleen first because she felt bad for him and then, later, because she was not able to get away?

He forced himself to open his eyes and face the sunlight. It hurt, but that could not be helped. He would have to hurt, if he was going to find a way to put Noahleen's needs first.

In full sunlight, the stairwell's gunmetal glare boomed loudly in Clay's eyes. It would be so easy just to tip himself forward and let his weight be swallowed by it. For a moment, his mind's eye cycled through different patterns of tumbling bodies bouncing down the stairwell. He saw a thousand ways that he could land, but he could not tell which ones were the most severe.

If he were to do this, it would have to be either death or bruising. Anything in the middle would be too terrible a burden to put on Noahleen. It would kill her if he wound up paralyzed or severely hurt and she had to take care of him. It would stress her until the seizures came back, rolling one over the other until her strength gave out and her brain cooked in its own fever. Clay could see that happening, someplace between his pain and the loud light.

He watched her collapsing in a thousand different ways from a thousand burdens he had put on her back.

If he made this choice now, it was the same thing as choosing to do that to her.

That thinking made him feel small, and the feeling angered him. It angered him more to realize that he was feeling cheated of the chance to hurt himself. He was revolted by himself, and his body shook as he tried to get away from his own consciousness.

Clay would never know whether he vomited first or whether he punched the door first. To him, they were just an instant during which his front became wet and he had a terrible, sudden certainty that the door was solid steel because his right hand exploded into a hot ball of agony that hung limply from his wrist.

Struggling to cope with the realization that he had just hurt himself, purposefully, in a way that might keep him from working to support Noahleen, Clay tried to shut out the gut-wrenching screams that filled the stairwell. When he started to feel lightheaded, he realized that they were coming from himself.

The bolt on the door turned. Clay reached out for the doorknob, desperate to force his way back inside before the lock clicked into place. When his fingers closed around it, though, his entire arm lit up with agony.

The bolt turned again, and a moment later the door was open. Noahleen fell onto him, at once massaging and pulling and trying to soothe him even as she tried to get him into the privacy of their living room. How long that took, Clay had no way of knowing. Time did not exist for him any longer. His world was the pain, and the pain was where his hand used to be.

Clay spent the rest of the day on the living room floor. There was no way for him to sit up without setting off fresh waves of chaos.

Noahleen spent the day alternating between overzealously anticipating needs he never had and pleading with him to go to the emergency room.

He could not do that, though. The money just was not there. Whatever was broken, Clay was sure it would be in the fine bones that could not be splinted anyway. The emergency room could not create a cast for this kind of break; doctors there would just charge him for x-rays and refer him to a surgeon that he could never afford.

So Clay stayed on the floor. He took aspirin and he forced his fingers to work, even when he had to bite into a pillow to do so. Even when it made him nauseous to try. If he kept his hand moving now, he reasoned, he would retain his dexterity later.

He hated that it hurt Noahleen to watch him work through the pain. He hated it more, though, when he thought about how much it would wind up hurting her if he bankrupted them just because he was too immature to reel in his temper. The only thing he could do was work his fingers, keep his dexterity, and ignore the pain.

He was sure that eventually his brain would just get used to it, like if it was a bad smell.

❖ ❖ ❖

Resentments & Illusions

"I don't know what to do anymore," Clay said as he did his best to make eye contact with Dr. Williams. "The more I try to slow down and implement the strategies we're working on here, the less control I feel like I have over my life."

As soon as he finished speaking, he looked up at the ceiling. The relief that washed over him was soothing enough that, for a moment, even his broken hand stopped hurting.

"What in particular are you talking about, Clay?"

The doctor did not miss a beat with her response. She was obviously poking him to get him to move in a certain direction. The only question was: which direction?

"Well, Noahleen for instance. I feel like not all that long ago I was a whole lot better at putting her feelings first than I am right now. Some of our recent arguments, they unfold like I'm watching them happen to someone else. I'll know that I should put aside my work or turn off the TV to talk, but even as I'm thinking about doing it, I start throwing things and screaming. It's embarrassing, because it's like I haven't even had time to decide whether or not I want to argue with her. My body just takes over and starts throwing a tantrum."

"That's disturbing," Dr. Williams said. She wrote a lot on her pad, then looked up at Clay. "Do you resent her for making you break your hand?"

Clay froze. Something was wrong with the question, but for a moment he could not put his finger on what it was. While he tried to sort it out, his mouth resolutely refused to open. He could not even deflect the question with an unrelated comment—he was simply speechless.

"Let's try this... What happened before the fight?"

Finally, Clay realized that Dr. Williams was trying to find out if he was hurting himself. He wondered what she would do with the information if he told her that he had done this to himself, that it was an accident but not really because he did it to stop himself from trying to die on the stairs.

Scenes from old television shows and movies played in his brain: Winston Smith attached to the pain machine in 1984. Picard in a similar position in "Chains of Command". How had he missed the fact that his favorite Star Trek episode had plagiarized the third act from *1984*?

He saw the institution in *Awakenings*, the old people's home in *Cocoon*, the cells from *The Count of Monte Cristo*, the morgue from *The Jacket*.

He was suddenly very aware that he might be in the most dangerous place for people like him—that he might have volunteered to allow his freedom to be contingent on a woman he did not know, who had formed her ideas about him from reports by other people that he did not know.

The place where the small bones in his right hand used to be burned. Clay looked down. He had wrapped the wrist, just to support it, but even with that and even with the swelling it was pretty obvious that the hand had no knuckles left intact.

He wanted to hide his injury from her gaze, but something told him that that would only make things worse.

"I need you to answer the question, Clay."

She was staring now.

He felt the panic start to rise in the back of his throat like bile. His whole right arm burned now, and even though it burned and it hurt and he wanted it to stop, he could feel it starting to rise. Clay knew that it was about to wheel back and strike, and he knew that if that happened, he would only aggravate the break. Maybe then he would make it bad enough that he really would need to go to the emergency room.

The worst part would be that he would not be allowed to go to the emergency room even then, because Dr. Williams would no doubt call the police. People like Clay had to be a professional hazard of some kind for her—he doubted very much that she was oblivious to the volatile situations that could arise when she spent her professional life alone with a series of men in dire situations.

No. He needed to get that hand under control before he wound up with an aggravated fracture and a jail sentence. Clay looked at the plaster wall. He would probably feel just as good punching the wall as he would punching Dr. Williams. He would probably wind up just as locked up too, though. She could always force him into a 48 hour observation if she wanted to do so.

Clay sucked his teeth and dug the nails of his left hand into the swollen flesh in the palm of his right hand. As he did this, he pinched and wiggled the inflamed area where small pieces of his metacarpals still swam loose. Two tiny chunks of bone sat in a pocket of soft tissue.

He could feel them. A second later, he was pinching the flesh and grinding these bones against each other. His feet kicked involuntarily when the pain washed over him, and he slumped in his chair with a heavy sigh.

It was the worst pain he had ever felt, and it was better than sex. The realization of that made Clay feel a little queasy.

Dr. Williams stared at him and pulled her brow into a dark "V". When she noticed he was looking back at her, she arched an eyebrow. He pulled himself up in his chair.

"Injuring my hand was an accident," Clay said. "I was trying to do something else, and I wound up slamming it by mistake. I'll admit that it might have happened because my attention was elsewhere, and that might be because my situation with Noahleen is spiraling out of control. And that might be because I'm having trouble at work. And the only thing that's changed at work is that I'm trying to do the things that you say will make it easier to get along, except that the stress is making me generally irritable and students are complaining about my mood swings and saying I'm treating them unfairly."

He was out of breath when he stopped talking. It was hard, but he had managed to get it all out in one shot, without pausing, so that he would not have the chance to get embarrassed and stop.

Dr. Williams wrote on her pad for a long time. Clay used that time to worry about whether he would get to go home to Noahleen or not. Dr. Williams had a private practice in an office building that she shared with an insurance agency, but Clay still felt like there might be large men in white hospital uniforms on the other side of the door, just waiting for her to call them in.

He took deep breaths, fully aware that what he was feeling was irrational paranoia. It was agony to be this self-aware and yet to not to be able to stop his brain from doing some of these things. The inside of his head felt like it was burning, just like his hand burned, and Clay cringed because he knew that both sensations were caused by things he was doing to himself.

He tried to regroup, but wound up huddled in his own mind, trying to avoid the parts of himself that liked this feeling. Clay wished Dr. Williams would give him something to respond to. At least then he would be able to put his own worries behind him, even if it was only to concentrate on whatever she wanted him to do.

Finally, the doctor cocked her head and said, "I think you're trying to make this about Noahleen because you're uncomfortable talking about your hand."

Clay sucked his teeth. His fingers found that tender spot on the palm of his right hand again. He let them linger there, but he forced himself to talk instead of toying with the injury.

"I think you just want to pick on me about my hand because you're not interested in whether or not your little exercises are working," he said. "In fact, you really haven't been interested in much other than walking through these behavioral routines and asking the same questions repeatedly until I change my answers. What's going on with that?"

He felt himself separating again, like he did when he picked fights with Noahleen. This time, though, instead of watching himself act out against his own will, he felt like he was watching someone use his own voice to stick up for him. It felt good, but it bothered Clay that he was still just a core of trembling fear watching his body interact with the world. He wanted to be the one in charge of what was happening, and knowing that he was not made him fearful, even when things seemed to be going well.

Still, he was happy to hear such strength in his own voice when he said things like: "So you're not going to answer? Only you get to ask the questions, is that it?"

Dr. Williams set her pad down on the floor. "What is it you want me to say?" she asked. "Do you want me to be your talk therapist and to tell you that you're doing well? Do you want to draw new lines and say our goals are to work on your mother issues or your social anxiety? We can do those things, but then I'm not going to be treating your autism, and it was my understanding that you came to me to treat your autism. Otherwise, there are plenty of relationship counselors and therapists I can refer you to, and then I can use my time to help a patient that wants to get better."

"I want to get better!" Clay yelled. "I want to feel good, to be able to walk into a room without worrying how bright the lights will be. I want to feel good without losing control of my arms, and I want to be able to feel bad without my clothes pulling tight around me. What the hell does that have to do with making eye contact and saying someone's name so they know I'm talking to them? How does that help? I'm trying to find out how to stop suffering, and you're playing Miss Manners."

Suddenly, he was not the scared core consciousness watching some other force use his body. Instead, he was living in his eyes, and those eyes were drilling themselves into Dr. Williams's face, refusing to blink, refusing to give way. This was not uncomfortable for him, but he could see her twisting. He used his drillbit eyes to ravage her face, searching for any line or furrow in her skin that he could use to accuse her of working against his best interests. Was this the way other people felt? Was this why they seemed so capable all the time?

Dr. Williams looked at the floor. Clay tried not to gloat. He just said: "That's what I thought. We're done here."

Then he stood up and walked to the door. When he grasped the handle, he heard Dr. Williams clear her throat, so he paused.

"If you go, don't ask for a referral," she said. "Don't transfer your files. Don't come back. If you have anyone try to contact me to verify your treatment or to approve your disability, I will be forced to tell them that you are non-compliant, and that I suspect you're a danger to yourself because you engaged in self-injurious behavior. If that happens, then I will have no choice but to include my observations about the extent of your injuries. Now we're done here."

Clay nodded, even though she could not see him. Her reaction was completely unsurprising. After doing nothing to help him for the better part of two months, it only made sense that she would insist on doing nothing to help him find another doctor.

He turned the door handle, smiling to himself as his broken hand lit up with pain during the effort. Then, sucking his teeth once again, he forced the fingers to grip. Inside himself, he squirmed as the pain tickled his mind, making it sharper and faster. The agony balanced the chaos he normally had to work to filter out of his consciousness. It was like a skilled orator.

Clay realized that now was the time that he learned to work with what he had, because no one was going to give him anything else. If his hand was broken, it still needed to work. If pain brought clarity and more than a little relief, then he would stop hating himself for it and start using those feelings strategically.

For the first time in years, Clay felt like he was in control of his life, and he wondered why he had let himself fear pain so much. It was fear, not pain, that had been damaging to him. It was fear that had pulled him outside himself and made him feel like he was not his body. Pain reminded him that he was his broken hand, that he could not watch himself do things. That the separation from himself had merely been an illusion caused by his fear.

❖ ❖ ❖

The Lure of Cold Metal

Clay watched himself in the mirror. He did not think that he looked unstable, just sad. Slick channels of tears cut through the foamy beard made by his shaving gel, but otherwise he was just a person. Anyone who watched his bathroom habits would think so.

Why, then, did he have such a hard time? Why was it that looking at his own face made him tremble and his fingers twitch, leaving him with the urge to slip the razor free of his Merkur 27?

It had only been a day since he felt good. Since he felt in control. He tried to force his mind back there, to that place it had been when he walked away from Dr. Williams. It would not go, though. That place was as far from the bathroom and the mirror as his childhood was from his marriage to Noahleen.

Why did he feel like carving hatch marks into his arms and legs? It had been years since he had done it. Hell, it had even been years since he had the urge to do it. The events of the last few days had unlocked those urges, though. That bright certainty that came to him when he provoked the wound in his hand also made him remember how easy it had been to smile, to look at people, and to get along in their world whenever he opened himself up with a boxcutter.

He knew that part of his impulsiveness was from the way that the constant pain would smother the chaos of his everyday environment like a wet blanket, muffling everything that might make him itch or that might distract him. That made it attractive.

It being secret made it more attractive. Not just because the pain worked—if it was just that, then his broken hand would be the end of his troubles. It would likely continue to hurt for months, and if tendinitis or arthritis developed, then he might find himself with a permanent focal point for his sensory environment. No, if the only problem was that Clay needed pain, then the urge to slip into that space where only the razor and his skin existed would never have risen, because he had other, better ways to make himself feel pain.

Instead, the razor was attractive precisely because it was transgressive. It was a way of marking up the difference between himself and everyone else. Even if he had to hide the razor marks, he knew they were there. Being marked in that way let Clay know that his rejection of the values, the ideas about what was right and wrong, and the assumptions about how people must feel about things like touch and sound and agony was real, and it was permanent. The scabs and scars reminded him that his commitment to himself was not like the paranoia and the imaginary problems that made him fearful. It was real.

He set the Merkur down on the bathroom counter. There was no way that he was going to use his broken hand to shave his face, not today. Not with the trembling he was having. Definitely not with the awful temptation that kept snaking its way back to the front of his mind whenever he suppressed it.

Clay watched himself in the mirror, imagining that his shaving foam beard was gone. He imagined rivers of bright red blood flowing down his cheeks like tears instead, and scars after those rivers dried. The mirror faded out of his perception, and instead he saw himself at work, having to explain these strange, oddly curving cuts that ran the length of his face. No one would believe they were accidental.

Could he claim he'd been assaulted? The slashes would be too narrow and too shallow to be from a fight. People would never believe that they were from a fight. Especially not when they took his size and his build into account.

No. Anyone who wanted to fight Clay would stab him in a way that disabled his will to fight back. Shallow slashes at his face would only make him angry. Everyone would see that; they would see right through whatever weak excuses he made.

He looked back down at the razor on the counter. No, he told himself, today was not a day that he should be worried about his five o'clock shadow. He knew that. He knew that when ghosts of other times and places came into the mirror, he needed to retreat.

The question was where could he retreat to? Being alone was obviously not good for him right now. If he clung to Noahleen, though, she would want to know why. She would think that he needed to talk through things. Noahleen was like that. She believed that you could only process feelings by speaking them out loud. That was why she did not understand about the mirror or the razor.

Would she be understanding about his falling out with Dr. Williams?

It had been an entire day and Clay had still not told Noahleen about that. Waiting had seemed like the right thing. It was supposed to give him the chance to calm down, to figure out how to tell her. Instead, the time begat more time. The longer he waited, the longer he found himself thinking he needed to wait. The awful truth of the situation was that Noahleen would be less understanding with each passing day, and he knew that. At the same time, though, he was worried about her not being understanding right away. How much worse could it get if he just waited—or if he said nothing at all?

Well, in that case he knew it could get pretty bad. The question was really how to tell her.

Ever since his diagnosis, their conversations had been about his coping strategies, his adaptations, his skills, and his ability to hold a job. She was only a couple years out from a major hospitalization and brain surgery of her own, but because he was the one who would ultimately be paying their bills, she had focused on making sure she was there to support him. It was no wonder that she was cracking up now, and it was unfair that he still was.

If she was going to hate him for walking away from therapy, then she might have a very good reason to do so. He had to admit that to himself, but admitting it just made him feel more anxious, more undeserving...

More in need of the cold release that came when open wounds felt the sting of air. The Merkur in front of him beckoned.

Clay turned his back on the mirror. He walked out of the bathroom and into the bedroom without wiping his face, lying down on the bed with his shaving foam beard still dripping off his cheek.

Noahleen was outside, taking her walk. He would have to find the energy to rise and to wash himself up before she got back. That, or he would have to come clean with her.

Clay forced himself to get back up out of the bed. He needed to find a towel.

❖ ❖ ❖

Dreams Filled With Razor Blades

Clay awoke panting and feeling an urgency that he could not place. His entire body twisted into knots around itself, searching for something. Something that had been there. He felt himself throbbing, his member swinging like a dowsing rod. What was happening?

Then he felt her hand behind his knee. It rarely touched him there. As soon as he realized that it was touching him, though, it was gone. It landed again on the outside of his left thigh. Something warm enclosed his member, and it stopped swinging.

While her hand butterflied over his stomach and up his chest, his mind tried to form a mental picture of what was happening, to map her body in relationship to his. When that proved to be too confusing for his sleepy brain, it settled for making him feel smothered. Suddenly, her hand was not teasing, it was pinning him in place, and when he tried to pull away, it pursued him. His whole body twitched, trying to bury itself in the mattress, to pull away. He could not breathe.

Noahleen's mouth—he could tell it was her mouth now—felt threatening on him. This was not right. He liked this. He told himself so.

Clay's body disagreed. He told his body to shut up and waited for it to comply.

His leg jerked. He heard an angry moan, then he was free as she pulled away from him. A trail of drool spread down his leg to his knee, but Noahleen stopped touching him.

"What the fuck?" She was angry.

Clay did not want her to be angry.

"I'm sorry," he said. "I startled awake."

"Bullshit you did," she said. "You were responding to me for a while. I understand if you're still mad at me because of your hand, but you don't have to try to break my jaw."

Clay sighed. He wished that Noahleen could start a fight normally, without saying something that was so loaded with assumptions that it required unpacking. He was tired, and he did appreciate what she was trying to do, but the weapon that she had just hurled at him was more potent and stealthier than her nighttime blowjob had ever had a chance to be.

Pain flared in his right hand, and then Clay realized that he was holding himself up off the bed with it. He laid back down. His hand went silent again. Fighting with Noahleen in the dark was frustrating. It gave his body too many opportunities to surprise him with its movements.

Light filled the room. Clay, on his back, squinted as five light bulbs flashed into being right in the center of his vision.

"Would you just fucking stop?" He shouted. "This is goddamned chaos."

He looked over toward the spot where the light switch should be. Noahleen stood, eyes wide and naked, with one hand on the dimmer switch. Her stomach was sucked in like she'd just taken a deep breath and she was about to speak, but she did not move.

"Just slow down," he said. "I have no idea what's happening or what your problem is. I'm still trying to figure it out."

Her body slumped as she exhaled and turned to face him.

"Okay," she said. "I should have realized that your stuff could still do stuff when you're asleep. I was just trying to surprise you."

"I'm surprised."

"Okay. It's just, you've been so stressed out since you got hurt. Well, even before that. I know I haven't made it easier."

This hurt more than the razor would have hurt. Clay twisted in bed, his limbs curling on him as his agitation sought a physicality that he did not want to give it.

"I don't need you to worry about me," he said as he twisted. His right hand screamed at him again. He sucked his teeth.

"Yes you do," she replied. "And I'm sorry I don't do it right."

She sat next to him on the bed, but she did not touch him.

"I just know things are going to be touch and go with the hand for a bit, so I wanted to do something just for you. I should have asked first."

"I don't need that," Clay said, "but I appreciate it. I just don't feel much like being touched these days."

"And I'm worried because that's never happened before. Not with me," she replied. "You'll have to excuse me for thinking that there might be a deeper issue between us."

Her voice grew hard as she kept talking.

"I'm not used to any of this, and I know you've been trying, but… you used to tell me everything, and even when you didn't, I was there for everything. You didn't have therapists and work friends and students that you spent all day with. It's hard not to get jealous and see threats around every corner when I feel like I'm trapped in the house and you're free to run around doing whatever. I didn't feel this way a month ago, or even six months ago, but lately… lately you've been spending a lot more time staring off into space instead of telling me what you did all day. It's like having conversations with a wall, sometimes."

Clay's chest tightened. He had decided to keep his separation from Dr. Williams a secret from Noahleen, at least for now. He was sure that she would try to get him to patch things up with the doctor, and he wanted to stave off that conversation. She had been the one who insisted that they find room for it in the budget, after all.

Then again, without Dr. Williams sucking up their disposable income, he could maybe save up for a surgery to fix his hand. Noahleen might be able to see the logic in that.

"What's this?" she asked, her fingers once again tracing his thigh.

Clay sat up carefully, making sure that he only used his left hand.

There were scratch marks all over his thighs.

"I didn't do this," Noahleen said. "When did it happen?"

Clay shook his head. He could not remember anything like this happening. Then he saw the same scratch marks on his forearms.

"It's like you're clawing yourself up in your sleep," Noahleen said. "Are you itchy or something? Having nightmares?"

Clay shrugged. "I guess it's one of those things."

"If this keeps up, promise me you'll go to urgent care to see a doctor about it."

"He'll just want to talk about my hand," Clay said.

"Yeah, well, if you have a weird skin condition it might be contagious. I can't afford to catch it—the pills give me a funky immune system, remember?"

Clay laid back on the bed again.

"Fine," he said. "Get the light, will you? I'll check for a rash in the morning, but it's not itching now."

The light blinked off. Clay was asleep again before Noahleen even got back into bed. That night, his dreams were filled with razor blades.

❖ ❖ ❖

Disclosure

The email from Dr. Kalkaska that summoned Clay down to her office for a meeting had not been terrible, but Clay noticed that it had not been particularly friendly either. In it, she indicated that the department head would sit in with them, which was normal for a performance review, but the fact that this performance review was happening in the middle of the semester made Clay nervous. It would make more sense to review him at the end of the semester, when the previous semester's student evaluations were available. Or perhaps they should have done it over the summer, before extending his contract. Not in the middle of the semester, though.

There was nothing about the idea of getting feedback that was directly troubling to him, but he could not help the feeling that there was something particularly wrong about the timing.

Once, Clay had known an adjunct professor who had been fired. In that case, there had been no private meeting. The department head at the time, Dr. Smith, had waited outside the classroom for the adjunct to show up, and then he had informed her that she would not be continuing to teach the class. He had brought a copy of the union contract for adjunct instructors with him and showed her the parts she was believed to be violating. She had a chance to talk to the union representatives and the right to a hearing, he had said, but she could not go back into the classroom until the situation was resolved. Then he had taught her class.

Clay had seen it all happen from a bench nearby. He was sure that he would have been asked to leave and give them some privacy, except that he had his headphones on, and for some reason people tended to overlook his presence more often when he had his headphones on. What people usually did not realize, though, was that Clay rarely had music playing on his headphones. Mostly, he just wore them to stifle background noises.

Clay was sure that he had not done anything that was so bad that they would take him out of the classes he was currently teaching—Dr. Kalkaska had, after all, taken his side (kind of) when the students complained about his quizzes. Also, there was the fact that Clay paid a great deal of attention to what his union contract did and did not allow him to do. Still, there was no reason why the department would want to renew a contract for a teacher whose students were constantly haranguing the higher-ups with complaints.

He worried that he would not be offered a new contract at the end of the year. He had always been worried about that, really, and every time a student became confrontational with him, he felt paralyzed by the idea that if he did not make the student happy and send her away, then she would complain until the department saw him as a nuisance and fired him. That it had not happened in three years did not affect Clay's fears. This mid-semester performance review that came immediately after a student complaint against him and involved the department head? That did affect his fears. It made them very strong and a little self-righteous.

This was Clay's interior state when he walked into Dr. Kalkaska's office and found that she and the department head, a new hire—Dr.

Smith having retired a few months ago—were already there and talking.

"Please sit down, Clay," she said, indicating an empty chair next to the department head.

"Hello, Clay," he said.

"Hello," Clay said as he sat. He tried to remember the man's name, but it evaded him.

"So," Dr. Kalkaska said as she tented her fingers, "we decided that we should do this evaluation now for a couple of reasons. For starters, we forgot to do one last year before Dr. Smith retired, so you're past due. There was also the issue with your class walking out a few weeks back."

Clay took a deep breath and waited for the axe to fall.

"We're not blaming you for that. Each and every professor here, from the newly minted part-timer to Dr. Brown himself," at his name, the department head nodded, "has experienced something like this. Sometimes, it's because we made a mistake or miscalculated the temperature of the room. Other times, it's because the students themselves are experiencing some issue that we're unaware of. It's not productive to talk about what the causes of an individual walkout are. What's productive is talking about some best practices for managing them."

Clay nodded. Then he realized he was holding his breath and he exhaled.

"Thank goodness," he said. "I have to admit, I've been a bit worried about that."

Dr. Kalkaska smiled. "You wouldn't be worth keeping in the department if you didn't worry when something like that happens. We keep hiring you because you think about how to improve your teaching methods."

Clay smiled. He still felt nervous, but there was no point continuing to keep a poker face if they were not going to go hard on him.

Dr. Brown spoke next.

"We do have some other concerns that need to be addressed alongside this discussion, though. A few people, both staff and students, have noticed that there seems to be a lot happening with you all at once. The issue with the class walkout, that—" he indicated Clay's hand. It was still swollen, but there were obviously no knuckles left intact. "—and there have been some behavioral things, too."

"Like what?" Clay's anger flared. Someone had been spreading rumors about him.

"A graduate student was in her office on the weekend and heard you having a very vocal argument with someone she assumed was your girlfriend. That's none of our business, but if she could hear it down the hall and around the corner, then…"

"Then we start to get concerned," Dr. Kalkaska finished. "Clay, we're not here to make trouble for you. You're an alum, you're a good teacher, and we know you've had a rough time with Noahleen being sick while you were in grad school. What we want is this: we want you to speak up if you're getting overwhelmed. We want to be able to put you in touch with resources, and to help you keep growing as a teacher. That means that you can come to us if you have an incident. You don't have to wait until a student complains."

"Now," Dr. Brown said, "is there anything we need to know about?"

Clay could feel both of their eyes on his hand, and he could feel his hand throbbing in response to the scrutiny. What he wanted more than anything was to scream, punch the desk, and walk out. Not because he was mad, but because he had no words for what he was feeling and he could not figure out how to calmly extract himself from the situation. He was trapped, and even though he knew that there was a way through this problem, he felt the temptation to cut himself loose regardless of the consequences.

"Well?" Dr. Kalkaska asked. "Is there anything we can help you with?"

Clay wanted to say that he was uncomfortable with the question. He wanted to say that he was pretty sure that they were not supposed to ask him about a medical issue, even if it was an obvious one like a broken hand.

He did not say either of those things, because he was ashamed. The attention that was being given to his hand was making him remember how he broke it, and he knew that he did not want anyone else to know how hopelessly lost he was capable of becoming. Something in him was sure that if they ever found out, they would not be as supportive as they were promising to be.

He waited for one of them to move the meeting forward, but it started to become obvious that they were not going to speak until after he responded to what they had already said.

"I'm, uh, that is, it's obvious…" Clay was having a hard time figuring out what he wanted to say, but the silence was too uncomfortable for him to allow it to continue. "I mean to say, you can't miss the fact that I have a broken hand."

Both Dr. Kalkaska and Dr. Brown nodded.

"And, I guess that would mean that I needed some accommodation under a lot of circumstances. For instance, I can't hold a pen right now."

They nodded again.

"Um, but I guess it's good that I mostly teach with computers then. Because I do have finger movement." He wiggled his fingers to show them. "So I can type. And, of course, I can stand up and talk."

He nodded.

"Okay," Dr. Kalkaska said. "But is there anything else you feel we should know about? How are you doing on your job search? Any luck finding a full time position?"

Clay shook his head.

"I'm not really looking at this point. I mean, I was, but I spent all my spare time trying to interview for positions and running around like a chicken with my head cut off, and I just can't really deal with that any more. I did find a couple of online schools that I'm teaching for on the side, so you know, I'm teaching a full time load. I just don't have the free time to teach that much and still keep traveling for interviews and searching job listings. Not with, you know, some of the other stuff I have going on."

Dr. Kalkaska nodded. Dr. Brown looked confused.

"That's unfortunate," he said. "If you need a reference, I would be happy to review your employment files, and then—"

"I'm autistic."

"Really?" Dr. Kalkaska's voice was incredulous. "But we've been working together for half a decade. I was your thesis advisor. How—"

"I know, right?" Clay caught himself nodding at high speed. "Right? And how did my parents miss it? And where were my counselors in high school? And how did I pass the university's admissions exam without remedial classes?"

Dr. Brown and Dr. Kalkaska looked at each other. Clay barreled forward.

"Part of the problem is that I wasn't diagnosable as a kid. Kids are taken care of, and the definition of the diagnosis didn't include me. And it was the eighties, so only crazy people saw therapists back then, because we hadn't figured out that everyone is crazy yet. Oh, and no one can tell that a little kid with no friends has problems with social language, because since he has no friends, he doesn't have anyone to use the social language with, right?

"But maybe, maybe I wasn't really a genius. Maybe I didn't spend all my time talking to adults because I was so smart that other kids didn't interest me. Maybe, I talked to the adults because they were always polite to me and because I didn't know about the power difference that made it weird for me to walk up and address adults as my equals. And maybe knowing that would have made a difference."

Clay suddenly realized that he had stopped trying to look at the other two people and had looked out the window instead. He stopped caring.

"I don't interview well. And I don't know that I can deal with office politics. I like to teach. I like talking to people about something I'm good at doing. I can do that. I don't know that I can do the other stuff, though. The stuff that involves arguing with other faculty. I just want to teach classes. And my therapist told me that I should keep this to myself because you wouldn't want to do anything to help me out, but she was kind of an idiot, so I refused to keep seeing her.

"I don't want to talk about my hand except to say that I'm autistic and I don't have health insurance and sometimes I don't know whether I'm hurt or not until it's way, way past time to do something about it. That's great if I'm trying to power through a 10k run or set a new max on my bench press, but it kind of sucks if I fall down the stairs or if I get the flu."

He slumped back in his chair, exhausted, and then he realized what he had just said. It was out there now—whether they accommodated him or not, they would always know.

Clay felt like he might need to vomit. At the same time, though, he felt happier than he had in a long time. He knew that what he had just done was a good thing, even if it meant that they would no longer let him teach his class.

Dr. Brown stood up.

"This is going to require Human Resources' intervention. Clearly, Clay, you are more than qualified to keep teaching. That does not change. You've been teaching successfully since you were a graduate student, and you've more than proven yourself. I'll be the first to admit that I don't know a thing about your condition, though. I'm also not very good at understanding what we're responsible for when it comes to disabilities—that's all H.R. I don't think there's much point, though, in continuing this meeting until we can reconvene with one of their people at the table."

Dr. Brown finished speaking and walked out without waiting to hear Clay or Dr. Kalkaska's reactions. When he was gone, Dr. Kalkaska cocked an eyebrow at Clay.

"I appreciate that you wanted to keep your medical issues private," she said, "but if you were planning on disclosing, I wish you would have told me so that I could help make it smoother for you."

Clay shrugged. "I didn't plan on it. I just didn't want to lie and you weren't going to move off it until I talked, so it kind of came out."

"Well I don't know what's going to happen next," she said. "We've never really had to have one of these meetings before. No one else on staff has disclosed a disability."

"Never?"

Dr. Kalkaska shook her head.

"There are a few older professors with hearing aids, but no one thinks of them as disabled. They're just old."

"So what do we do now?" Clay asked.

"We go home, and we wait until Human Resources tells us what we have to do," Dr. Kalkaska answered.

Clay thought about what Dr. Kalkaska's last statement might mean. Then he swallowed his gorge, smiled, and excused himself from her office.

❖ ❖ ❖

Heavy Hand, Light Touch

Cartoon faces hovered in Clay's field of vision. They looked familiar, but he could not place where he had seen them before. When he tried to look away, though, they moved with him. When he closed his eyes, they were there, projected against the back of his eyelids.

What did they mean?

"Tell me what you think the person on the left is feeling," a voice said. The voice was familiar, too.

Clay strained to focus on just the face on the left. It was frowning, but the frown was not very big. The one on the right was smiling. He tried not to look at the one on the right.

"It's okay, take your time."

He squinted. Then he tried to close his right eye, so that he would only see the one on the left. Unfortunately, he could still see the one on the right, even with one eye closed.

Something was not right about this situation.

"Well?"

"I thought you told me to take my time," Clay replied.

"I did. I just wanted to check," the voice said back to him.

Clay focused in on the proper image. The brow was furrowed. The frown was not too deep, but there were lines around the eyes. He supposed it was a scowl, but that could mean that the person was annoyed or angry or frustrated. How was he supposed to know which it was?

He relaxed his concentration as he considered the options, and the image on the right, the smiling image, came back into his consciousness.

"Happy," he mumbled.

"You think the one on the left is happy?" the voice said.

Clay tried to say no, but he was too angry with himself for letting his control slip and saying something he did not intend to say. This kind of thing happened all the time, and he was mostly punished for sassing when it did, even though he had no idea what words had escaped his throat until a few seconds after they did.

When he opened his mouth to say "No, I accidentally looked at the right side," he heard himself scream "Fuck you! You're trying to trick me," instead.

Inwardly, he sighed. When this happened, he had no choice but to watch himself flail around and to wait for it to be over.

As he listened to his own voice pouring invective all over the person who had been talking to him, he wondered how it was that he had such a core of sober self-awareness. It often seemed like he was watching himself act out these tantrums, but usually he could still feel the physical sensations of air tearing through his vocal chords, the dizziness that came with the surges in adrenaline, and the impact as he threw his body against whatever immovable object was nearby.

This time, though, it was like he was in a bomb shelter. He felt nothing. It made him want to scream, so he did.

The cartoon faces dropped away and a balding, middle-aged man in a cheap brown suit replaced them. Clay recognized the face—it was the face of Mr. Weir, the counselor from his elementary school. It had been years since he'd even thought about Mr. Weir, let alone seen him. Here he was, though, standing right in front of Clay.

"I'm sorry, Clay. I just don't know what to do," he said. "I tried to talk to your parents about this, but they said you were just misbehaving. Apparently, you do this a lot, and you need to learn that it's not acceptable. Just stop doing it, okay? Just stop doing it, and then everyone can be nice to you, because you'll be normal."

Clay felt the scream this time. It was the scream he'd felt as a child, the one that ripped through his thoughts and made it impossible to talk. The one that made him stare at people until they punched him for being weird. Over the years, it had died down, but it was always there.

His knuckles burned. The broken bones in his hand rustled against each other, and he heard the scream pour out of the mess of clicking and grinding that they created.

Somehow, he was back in Dr. Kalkaska's office. Dr. Brown was there. Was he in the middle of another performance review? Or was this the follow-up he'd been promised?

Clay looked around, but he did not see the representative from Human Resources who was supposed to be there.

He opened his mouth to ask what was going on, but when he did, the scream poured out of him. He tried to close his mouth again, but the scream refused to be bitten in half. He gagged on it, which felt odd, because he had never gagged while something left his throat before.

Dr. Kalkaska and Dr. Brown both looked at him. Their gazes were blank, their faces emotionless. They opened their mouths together, and the scream poured out of both of them. Somehow, their scream allowed Clay to close his mouth. When he did, theirs opened wider, and the scream they emitted became louder. He watched in horror as their mouths continued to open wider and wider, until their heads flipped back like their jaws were hinges on the back of their necks. The scream poured upward out of them, like a spirit escaping their bodies and fleeing for the sky.

Clay shut his eyes against it. People's heads were not supposed to move that way.

"Here's my oldest daughter," he heard his father say.

He opened his eyes again. Mark Dillon stood in front of him. Another man was there, too. Clay did not recognize him, but he was wearing a suit.

"He's in the Boy Scouts, but if he keeps reading those Sailor Moon comics, I might have to get him a Brownies uniform," Mark said. "As it is, it's all I can do to keep him from wearing that black lipstick around the house."

The man in the suit chuckled. Clay looked down at himself. He was wearing his leather skirt and fishnet sleeves. He had no shirt on because his chest was covered with Nair. Nearby, the offending comic books were scattered all over the floor.

"It's not a gay thing," the man in the suit said. "Japanese people are just weird. Their cartoons are making our kids weird."

Clay opened his mouth, this time intending to scream. Nothing came out.

"Yeah, I'm sure it's just a phase," Mark said. "I just can't wait until it passes. You know he has a girlfriend? Some little lesbian wants to make out with that, even with all the David Bowie makeup."

"Anyway, if you come downstairs, you can see my son A.J. is working on our setup for breeding. He's a rascal—not too good at school, but he can get these reptiles to breed like it's nothing else. I actually got into the hobby because of him."

Clay watched as his father led the unfamiliar man out of the room. When they were gone, he found the scream. It tore through him until his skin turned brittle and shattered. It was an amazing feeling, because it allowed him to break loose from everything that felt constricting—his clothes, his father's expectations, even his skin.

I am my body, but I am not my body because my body does not feel like it's got all the parts it should have.

Who had said that? He could not tell.

He was no longer screaming. Now he was in the gym, and he was throwing punches while holding ten pound weights. Three more minutes of high-speed weighted kickboxing and then he could go to the exercise bike. He was almost done.

Then he remembered the ice cream he had eaten the night before, and he realized that he would need to add fifteen minutes on the stair-stepper to the end of his workout. Dammit.

At least Kelly was here. He wanted to fuck her so badly, but he knew he would never work up the willpower to cheat on Noahleen. Kelly had everything, though. She was muscular, but she still had those huge tits, and they never sagged. Her face was open, bright—when she and he traded stations on the weight machine, she was always courteous. She never shamed him for sweating more than the other guys did.

They had the same eye and hair color too. He wanted to fuck her so badly.

Suddenly, Clay realized that he did not know her. They'd never talked about anything except the gym equipment. He still wanted to be inside her, though. To feel what it was like, to know how living inside that perfection could be.

No. Wait.

Was he attracted to her or just jealous of her body?

Clay's entire being snapped to attention as his eyes popped open. He felt his leg connect with flesh and mumbled an apology. Then he realized that he was covered in sweat.

Noahleen's hand was on his chest.

"I'm sorry," she said. "I just wanted to check to make sure you were okay. You started screaming, and then you were punching the pillow with your bad hand and screaming 'no' over and over again."

"Dream," Clay said.

"I gathered that," Noahleen replied. "I was worried about you re-injuring yourself though."

He nodded. There were no words to follow it.

Noahleen pulled her hand away from his chest. He arched his back, following it, keeping that contact as long as he could. When she finally pulled back further than he could follow, he groaned.

The place where her hand had touched him felt like it was on fire.

"Okay," she said. "I don't get you sometimes, but okay."

The hand was back, and it was soft. He pressed himself up against it. The hand pressed back. He looked Noahleen in the eyes. It felt good to do that, for once.

It was funny, looking her in the eyes in the dark, because all he could see was the glint of reflected light along the right edge of each one. She seemed to know what he was doing, though—maybe she could see the white crescents of the reflected light at the edge of his own eyes? He had no idea.

Before he could ask, her mouth was on his. He felt like he was falling. It had been so long since they had kissed. At least, since they had kissed on the mouth. Their sex life generally did not involve much face-to-face time, and when they cuddled she usually gave him a cheek or a forehead or a hand.

Tonight was different. Tonight, she devoured his mouth. The hand on his chest slid to the side and groped his pectoral muscle. It squeezed hard, and he caught his breath.

"Those aren't toys, you know," he said.

She giggled.

"Stop being a girl," she said, but then he felt her mouth move to his nipple.

He decided to do the opposite.

She moaned as she worked him over, feeling, kissing, and kneading his body. The chaos of her movement made him twist. Was that her hand on his thigh? No, there was wetness, she was kissing the spot in his hip where his leg met his torso. Then something like a whisper danced on his nipples.

He felt himself getting hard, but she seemed to be avoiding his member, as if it would break the spell that her hands and lips were working.

His back arched.

Everything she had been doing to his body for several minutes started happening at once.

This time, when he screamed, there was no tearing sensation. There was no feeling of an external force ripping through him. This time, it was his entire body singing.

When the only parts of him still touching the bed were his heels and the back of his head, she moved her mouth down over him. All sense of space and distance went away. He closed his eyes against the little light left in the room. This let his nerves play the afterimage of Noahleen's work at high volume until suddenly there was nothing.

A second after there was nothing, cold air sheared across his member, chilling him in a way that made him strain, insistent.

Then there was weight. In the weight there was comfort. Then her hands were on his face, and he was warm again.

As Noahleen rocked her body up and down on him, he tried to reach forward. He wanted to touch her, to find those places on her body that she had tickled on his.

"No," she said, pushing his hands away. "You're not mauling me with your broken hand. You'll just hurt yourself."

He moaned and twisted.

"I said no!" This time there was iron in her voice.

Perversely, this made Clay want to ignore her. Instead of reaching out to caress her, he wheeled back and slapped her as hard as he could on the ass. With his good hand.

Because he still had his eyes closed, he never saw the punch that she threw back at him. He could feel that it was closed-fisted though. What surprised him was the moan that he let out when it happened.

"Sorry," she said. "I didn't mean to do that so hard."

He reached up and twisted her nipple. This time he used his broken hand.

"Fuck!" she yelled and punched him at the same time. "Goddamn it, I'm not trying to do that."

He chuckled.

His muscles warmed up and loosened, uncoiling like they did in the moments after he went to work with a razor blade. The pain from her punches radiated out from his cheek with a warmth that he suddenly needed more than he needed anything. This was his answer. This was the way he would feed the beast that screamed in his head and made him hit steel security doors.

He kept ignoring Noahleen's pleas for him to hold still. Each time he did, she pushed harder against him. Twice more, he tricked her into hitting him, and then he grabbed her, held her close, and refused to let her move.

The strain of not being able to ride him woke up whatever it was in her that went crazy when he tied her up and teased her. Her moans became deeper, until she was grunting, and she pushed back hard.

This time, when she hit him, it was open-palmed. Somehow, that hurt more.

He moaned.

"So that's how this is," she murmured. Then she slapped him again.

He retaliated by arching his back until she lifted off the bed. He impaled her, removing her ability to move back against him at the same time.

"Okay," she said. Something in her voice made him imagine that her eyes were rolled up into her head. "But now I need you to behave until I'm done."

Before he could say anything, he felt her hand gripping his throat. Her fingers sank into his muscle, but she did not choke him. Whenever he tried to move, though, she dug into the meat on his neck, using it to leverage herself back down on him. It made his face numb when she did that, and then he lost the will to defy her.

He made sure to move a lot, until he could not fight back any more, and then it was over.

Clay fell asleep while Noahleen's weight still pinned him to the bed. This time, he dreamed of nothing but floating on his back in a pool. Sunlight bathed his face. His ears were below the water line, so there was no sound.

He had never been so calm in his life.

❖ ❖ ❖

Facilitating Communication

The campus's quad spun around Clay as he hurried to class. Today was not the day for dealing with his work clothes bunching up and constraining him, which was probably why it was happening. Stress. Anxiety. He knew that everything would be better if he just excused himself to the bathroom to get re-dressed, but he was only three minutes from the start of class and he was still at least five hundred feet from the building's entrance. His class was on the fourth floor.

Dr. Brown would be observing that class today, as part of the ongoing evaluation of Clay's disability and needs. Clay was not sure that this was exactly how it was supposed to work, but when he raised questions about the process, Dr. Brown and Dr. Kalkaska were both quick to point out that he was past due for an in-class observation anyway, and that this was in no way singling him out.

Clay did not have to like the situation, he just had to live in it.

The nightmares last night were not what he wanted to carry into the day today. Nor was the sex, really. It had let him relax so that he could sleep, but his throat felt raw from the rough play and he was sure that he was walking in a way that broadcast the limp and wrung-out feeling in his limbs. Combined with the jittery nerves brought on by his nightmares, it made him feel like a mess, and Clay knew that he had a tendency to look exactly like he felt.

His dress shirt felt too tight across his shoulders. He squirmed, but he was almost running, so it threw his balance off. His left ankle rolled sideways as his weight came down on it.

Clay had to stop before he hurt himself even more. He set down his bag and took a few deep breaths, testing the strength of the ankle. Everything seemed okay.

He picked up his things and pressed on. Eventually, he made it into the building and up the stairs. It felt like forever while he was doing it, but he pressed on, telling himself to ignore everything that his brain was yelling at him.

Clay knew then: his brain was a liar, and it deserved to be ignored. The only issue for him was whether or not he was strong enough to ignore it. It was only when he stood in front of the class and opened his mouth to speak that he knew. He knew that words would come out, not screams, not sobs. He was successfully ignoring his brain.

He opened the class discussion and noticed as he did so that he was actually five minutes late. He scanned the room for Dr. Brown and smiled to himself when he realized that the doctor was also late. Clay smiled when he slipped in self-consciously at the back of the room. Dr. Brown must have thought the smile was a greeting, because he nodded and waved as he unfolded his body into one of the chairs at the back of the hall.

Clay continued his introduction of the day's material. His spirits were up; he was feeling focused.

Why had he worried? His stupid brain did not know what it was doing.

As he worked through the lesson, the fact that it was going so well started to eat at him. Clay absolutely wanted his performance review and classroom observation to reflect the best demonstration of his talent, but part of him kept pointing out that having such a good day could make Dr. Brown question Clay's need for accommodations. He tried to tell himself that what he was requesting were not in-class changes to the format so much as organizational and background support, but there was a terrified voice at the core of his being that kept shouting back at him that it did not matter.

He knew, too, why the voice was shouting so loudly. It was because most people make their judgments about others from what they see, not what they hear reported back. No matter how much anxiety Clay felt or how much he had to force himself to talk through it, his complaints would never be as credible as the sight of him calmly speaking before a large group of people. His ability to do was the direct enemy of his ability to be.

Clay stopped speaking and stood still as that thought unfolded in his mind. He saw concern flash across a few faces in the front row when he did. Behind that, though, the faces blurred with the glare of the room's lighting and made him dizzy.

He sat down to combat the dizziness, and then he heard a few people stand up.

"It's okay," he said. "I just got a little lightheaded for a moment."

He pushed himself back up to his feet. The voice was not him, it was just his stupid brain, and he needed to work through it.

"I must have rushed out the door without breakfast this morning." He hoped his smile was good enough to fool his students but not good enough to fool Dr. Brown.

Clay looked over at the projection screen on the right side of the stage, hoping that he was projecting something that would help him remember where he had just left off when he sat down. He had not been listening to his own speech, so he had no idea how far into the presentation he had been when he stopped talking. He saw that they were only on the third slide, something about JQuery bugs, and he knew what to do next.

Keeping the conversation on-track while his brain tried to make him sort out his feelings was difficult, but he kept it up for a while. The strain made him stutter, something he only rarely did when he was speaking from a prepared script, and that made him more self-conscious. Briefly, he let himself wish that he was allowed to just stop talking and to type the rest of his presentation on his laptop so that his students could read it off the projector and take notes.

Then it occurred to him that he might be able to do just that. Nothing he had ever been told about teaching said that it was off-limits. He had never seen anyone do it, but what did that matter?

For the second time in five minutes, Clay stopped talking. This time, more people stood up. He waved them down.

"Class is not over yet," he said. "But we are going to try something different."

He sauntered over to the podium and turned off the slideshow his laptop was projecting. Next, he opened up a blank document in his text editor and started to type.

"Take notes," he said. "I want you to see how this develops and why I choose to comment up the code, so that you can learn to do that."

With that, he typed for five minutes, setting up entire command strings and then reversing course to add explanatory comments to the script. Hands started to go up, but he put them back down by raising his finger and mouthing "wait." When he had filled the screen, he stepped away from his computer and said, "You can raise your hands to ask questions now."

Hands shot up. In the back, he could see Dr. Brown sit up straighter, but Clay could not make out the look on the older man's face because the glare from the projector was too strong.

Clay waved to the first hand he saw as he stepped back to the computer. As the student asked about the specifics of a three-line chunk, Clay typed the question and answer into his line comments. He saw other hands go down as he typed, and he heard the clacking-and-scratching sounds of people writing and typing notes throughout the room.

Slowly, silently, they built a dissected outline of the code segment together. Time inched forward more slowly now, but the quiet in the room made it easier to concentrate, so the molasses movement of the laptop's clock stopped bothering Clay. The world narrowed to his students' questions, his keyboard, and his code.

Finally, one person's question was "Can we go? Class was over ten minutes ago."

Clay nodded and thanked them for bearing with him. As they filed out of the room, he reminded them to email him if they had more questions as they did their homework.

Eventually, he was left alone in the room with Dr. Brown.

"Well," Dr. Brown said, "there was a bit of an abrupt transition in the middle of class there, but I think that your method for encouraging students to look at the code more closely is compelling."

Clay grinned. "You know what that was. We all have our off days—what matters is how we recover. It's like acting on stage," he said.

Dr. Brown nodded.

"This really was just routine," he said. "You should make a list of demands, though. I can tell you that the university is going to have you consult a therapist that works for an occupational and recovery-based service, and they are going to have someone in Human Resources reading my report and the shrink's report, and then they are going to offer you some choices. All I can tell you is that you should have your mind made up about what you want before they present those choices, because I don't know how well-informed or useful they will be. I wish I could say more."

Clay nodded. "I appreciate the advice," he said. "Honestly, I didn't know what you were thinking, and I've been terrified of this whole situation."

Dr. Brown shrugged. "Honestly, I don't know what I'm thinking I'd rather just let you do whatever you want, but if you go too far outside the students' comfort zone, then that can impact their ability to learn the material. If I had my way, we'd just tell you to do whatever you needed, and then we'd check up at three months, six months, and a year to make sure you are still delivering the course learning objectives.

Above my head, though, they look at hands-off management as just pure chaos. They don't see how it can work. So we're both going through a process right now. I just wanted you to have some perspective about that."

Dr. Brown excused himself then. Clay found himself unable to frame a verbal response in time to get the last word. Once he was alone, he realized that he was probably better off for it.

❖ ❖ ❖

Occupational Assessment

Clay was nervous about seeing the university's psychologist. He knew that the session was supposed to be an assessment of his occupational needs, and that it was a one-time interview, but he still felt as nervous as he had felt back when he walked in to the county's mental health clinic and told the receptionist that he was having a problem. That had been the beginning of the diagnostic process for Clay, but on the day that he asked for help, it had not felt like it. Instead, it felt like he was turning himself in. Like he knew he had finally been caught, and he was choosing to go peacefully.

Of course, on that day, he had not actually been detained. The receptionist had made an appointment for him to meet with a case worker so that they could get his information, and she had promised that the caseworker would be able to help Clay get an appointment. After she handed him his appointment card for the meeting with that caseworker, he had walked home. He had even been told before the fact that all he would get out of them on the first day was an appointment. None of that mattered, though. What mattered was that, in the moment, he was abdicating all control over his future to a faceless authority. And that he was choosing to do it because he could see no other way to continue surviving.

As he walked through the doors of the university's counseling and evaluation center, Clay felt the same way. He knew that he would not be committed or even held longer than the hour of his appointment, but he still felt like he was surrendering himself to the university. He was forcing some of the weight of his distress onto them, and letting them steer his future behavior to an extent. It was a frightening thing to do.

This time, at least, he already had an appointment, so he did not have to wait in the reception area until someone got to him. This time, he gave his name to the receptionist and, since it was university business, they escorted him right back to a cubicle where he could collect his thoughts while he waited. Being able to wait in solitude made everything easier somehow. He still wondered what exactly he would be expected to disclose, but at least he did not have to wonder what the people around him thought he was here for.

Clay sat for a long time, which surprised him because the receptionist had been so quick to move him back here. Maybe, he thought, the university just tried to avoid leaving its employees out with the regular patients because...

His thought trailed off as he realized that he could not think of a reason for anything that was happening, and that even if he could, he would probably be wrong.

At some point, a young blonde woman leaned into the cubicle and said, "Sorry for the wait. We don't have a regular occupational psychologist on staff right now, so we're waiting for a consultant to come and see you. Do you want anything while you wait?"

Clay asked for water to get the woman to go away.

He did not like this. It was one thing to say that the university was going to have one of their own evaluate him, but this whole idea of bringing in a stranger, someone who had no part in this whatsoever—

He forced himself to take a deep breath and then to admit that he was letting his imagination get away from him. Noahleen would have talked him down if she was around to see him escalate, and he wanted to keep calm, but when he felt the pace of his breath accelerating against his own best efforts, he knew he was failing.

Suddenly, his lungs opened wide, and instead of a couple of fast shallow breaths, Clay's chest swelled with air, expanding until his shirt was tight.

The deep breath helped. He held on to it. Within seconds, he could feel his body relaxing. He exhaled.

There was nothing to do but wait.

The young woman returned with his water then, and Clay sipped at it while he looked around the cubicle. The walls were mostly empty, except for a few tacks that said that they had once held... something.

Luckily, his wait was not much longer. The occupational psychologist pushed her way into the cubicle just seconds later, scattering her keys, purse, and other personal belongings in a whirlwind gesture that left her coat draped over the top of the cubicle wall. It also left Clay wiping the raindrops that the coat had shed off his face.

When he finished, he looked up at the psychologist.

"Hello, Clay," she said. "Can't you recognize me? It hasn't been that long since you stormed out of my office."

"Hello, Doctor Jeannie Williams," Clay said.

She stuck her hand out. "I'm glad to see you again," she said.

He took it. Her grip was firm, like he would have expected from a man. He pulled and winced as she worked one finger over the spot where his middle finger knuckle used to be.

"I see we're still working on allowing social touching," she said.

"No," Clay replied. "We're healing from a broken hand."

He held his broken hand up in front of her face and made a fist to show her that there was now a long depression between his index and pinkie fingers where two knuckles should have been.

"Ow," she said. Then she tried to look him in the eye. "How'd that happen?"

"I did it," Clay said, "on accident."

Dr. Williams nodded. "Okay," she said.

He lowered his fist.

"Why are you here?" he asked.

"The same reason you're here, Clay," she said. She smiled too much when she said it.

"No, I mean, aren't you breaking some sort of ethical guidelines? Do they know that I saw you? Or that I chose to discontinue treatment?"

"Absolutely not," she said. "Who do you think I am? I do this kind of thing for the university on a pretty regular basis. When they called about you, I volunteered to see you because of our history and because I would have had to submit your file to whoever they hired anyway. I thought you might appreciate it if I just came in person instead."

Clay harrumphed. This was not what he wanted, but what was he supposed to do?

"Look," Dr. Williams said, "I can go down the hall and communicate my notes about your case to someone else, and then I can send that doctor back down here. Or you can just do the interview with me, and then we don't have to complicate this with another person's assumptions about your condition."

"It's your assumptions I'm worried about," he said. "If I do this, are you going to listen? Or are you here to follow through on your promise to block my access to disability resources?"

"What?" she asked. She looked genuinely confused.

"When we first started, you said that you weren't going to do any disability paperwork for me. You repeated the threat when I wanted to stop seeing you. Is that why you're here? To prove to them that I'm not disabled?"

"No," she said, "and I don't think you're remembering everything that happened the right way."

"Don't try to lie to me," he said. "You told me you didn't want me to disclose to the university, and you told me that I wasn't really disabled and that you wouldn't do disability paperwork for me."

She took a deep breath and let it out. "Okay," she said. "I said on the first day that I wouldn't do paperwork for you because you were unresponsive, and every time I wanted to try something out, to roleplay or to work on your social skills, you just asserted your diagnosis from your last doctor. Then you shut down. I'm sorry I said it, but I was getting suspicious that you had only gotten a referral to me because you wanted someone to help you file for benefits. Since you were working and you were pretty successful, all things considered, I didn't want to encourage it."

"And after that?"

"After that, I don't know. When you left, I only said what I said to try to make you rethink the choice to take such an extreme action. I was surprised that you didn't try to reconnect. Why? What did you think was happening?"

"Well, let's see," Clay said, "I met you for the first time and you tried to tell me that I wasn't autistic. Then you told me that you wouldn't help me with disability and that we could handle everything I needed together. You didn't ask me what I needed first, though, did you? So I assumed that you had already decided everything you needed to decide about me before you met me. After that, it was just a matter of going through the motions and hoping you'd catch on. When seeing you got to be more stressful than not seeing you, I quit, and you used the opportunity to threaten me. Why?" he bugged his eyes out at her, "What did you think was happening?"

Clay threw himself against the back of his chair. The impact jarred his mind enough to keep him in the room and focused. He knew that he could not afford to let the anger run away with him here, but he also could not afford to suppress his emotions so much that he wound up staring off into space.

After a few seconds, Dr. Williams stopped trying to meet his gaze. She looked down at her lap instead.

"Okay," she said. "Now that you put it together for me, I can see how you connected those dots. I'm sorry." She looked up at him. "Would you be open to the idea that maybe you have something going on along with autism? I never meant to question your original diagnosis, but you have some other symptoms that are not autistic symptoms, and I think you might have another condition. Maybe it was a condition caused by the stress that came with..." she waved her hands as her voice trailed off, "...with coping with all these misunderstandings. Seriously. I didn't mean to make you think that I doubted your diagnosis. There's more going on with you than just autism."

He nodded.

"So let's get through this together," she said. "And then I want to talk to you about picking our therapy back up. Maybe you can talk to me about what it is that you were refusing to talk about in our sessions."

Clay considered her offer. He was still unhappy about the fact that he had been ambushed by Dr. Williams, but he could see where her interpretation of events came from, now that she had explained it to him.

"Okay," he said. "We can set up a follow-up appointment at your office."

"And then you'll be honest with me?" she asked.

Briefly, Clay considered it. He tried to imagine talking to Dr. Williams about the thoughts he had while he shaved himself.

The regrets that bubbled to the surface when he saw himself in the mirror surged now, threatening to take hold of his mouth and break free as words. He pushed them back down, swallowing hard to keep them in his gut.

"I won't lie to you," he said. "and I'll try my best."

"Okay, then," Dr. Williams said. "Let's talk about your work life. That's what we're here for. What stresses you out when you're in the classroom? What do you want from the university?"

Clay froze.

"Well?" Dr. Williams asked.

"I don't know," Clay said. "I really like teaching. I look forward to class every day. What is the usual thing to do in these circumstances?"

"Well, if you worked in a regular office that required you to be in attendance for eight hours each day, I might advise them to allow you to use headphones when you are doing tasks that require concentration. Or we might talk about how to streamline your work so that you can work from home on bad days. To eliminate environmental distractions. That way, you can be as productive as possible.

"Since your job involves public speaking, though, I don't know what to recommend. The university already lets you work from home. In fact, they prefer that you do, because you're only a part-time instructor and they can cram a bunch of you into the same office if no one actually uses that office. You're not required to go to any department meetings that aren't directly about your performance in the classroom, either, so there's nothing for me to argue that they should excuse you from.

"This is why I encouraged you not to disclose before. You're already in a job that's adapted to your needs. What else could you want?"

Clay thought about what Dr. Williams had said. She was right, but what she said still sounded wrong. He was here because he was having dreams about razor blades, he was unable to look at himself in the mirror without wanting to have a body that he could never have, and his broken hand was still slightly swollen from all of the times that he had re-aggravated the break in the course of his daily activities. There had to be something that he could ask for that would make his life better.

"I want access to health insurance," he finally said.

"I can't help you with that," Dr. Williams replied, her brow furrowed.

Clay waited for her to explain herself.

Finally, she said, "I can't make them offer you more benefits. I can't make them increase your salary. Those things are not part of this process. You understand that, right?"

Clay nodded. He knew that. Kind of. She had asked what he wanted, though.

"How fucked up is it," he said, "that I can be disabled, and I can also be capable of doing my job even though I'm disabled, but I can't access a doctor when I break my hand without going so far into debt that I have to eat cat food to make my ends meet?"

Dr. Williams remained calm, but her eyes got very wide. Clay stared at her. He knew that he should prevent himself from staring because it made people uncomfortable. He hated it when people stared at him. He still stared, though, because staring at her made him more comfortable, and he was sick of working around everyone else.

Dr. Williams was supposed to be his doctor. She was the only kind of doctor he could afford.

For once, he decided, someone else could be uncomfortable so that he felt comfortable.

After a moment, Dr. Williams said, "It's really fucked up, Clay. But I can't do a lot about it unless you're willing to give up your job. You make too much to get Medicaid, and you're not disabled enough to get an exemption unless you become too disabled to work this much."

Clay had expected her to say something like that, but hearing it still made his brain explode with rage. Before he knew what he was doing, he raised his broken hand and made a fist. Then he smashed it into the cubicle's wall as hard as he could.

Pain erupted into his eyes, flashing bright light that boiled in on itself. He knew then that he had re-broken his hand again, and that it would be at least two weeks before he could hold a pencil. Again. The light and the location of the pain, which felt like it was in the front of his brain and not in his hand, told him as much.

He cried because he knew that this kind of pain should not be so familiar to anyone.

Dr. Williams touched him on the shoulder and he recoiled, which smashed his back into the wall. More pain bloomed, but this time it was located in his shoulder and not in his brain. That was comforting.

After a few seconds, he realized that Dr. Williams was speaking to him. Her voice was unnaturally soft, softer than it had ever been before. He held on to the sound of her voice, hoping that it would eventually form words that he could understand.

"Is this how you first broke your hand?" she asked.

He nodded. He hated himself for admitting it, but he nodded. He lacked the strength to pretend any more. Besides, she had just seen him hurt himself.

"How often do you do this, Clay?"

"Really often sometimes, and other times not for years," he said. "I used to do it with razors so that I could avoid breaking my own bones, but I gave up razors ten years ago. I've been good since then, except for the last few months. I've been really good, but I'm not any more."

"You are being good, Clay. Look at everything you have. Look at what you've accomplished. If not for your wife's disability, you might have lived with autism your entire life and never known it because you would never have been tested in a way that put you into crisis. You are fine. I need you to talk to me about this, though. How many times have you broken your hand?"

Clay shook his head. "I don't know. That once, the time back when I was seeing you. It's been touchy since then, though. I think this is the first time I've re-broken it, but I've hurt it a few times on accident. Usually just from trying to lift with it when it's not ready. Once because I tried to play a video game.

"I don't like to punch things, it just happens."

Dr. Williams sat forward in her seat. "Have you ever punched another person, Clay?"

He shook his head. He could feel tears pooling up in his eyes again.

"You're sure?"

He nodded. "Once," he said, "I pushed Noahleen out of my way so that I could punch the bathroom door. She fell, and then I punched and kicked the door until it had holes in it because I was so disappointed in myself. Then she called me stupid because we couldn't afford to buy a new door and the whole house was going to smell like a toilet every time one of us made. That was the closest I got to hitting her. Ever."

Dr. Williams nodded. "What happened then?" she asked.

"I walked down to the gas station and bought a utility knife. Just a little one that went on a keychain. Then I used it to carve up my arms until I calmed down. I sat in my car while I did it so that Noahleen wouldn't know I was home again. I had to show her, though, because there was more blood than I wanted there to be and I couldn't get it to stop."

"And how long ago was this?"

"Ten years ago," he said. "I stopped cutting then because I was too afraid of killing myself. I didn't want to kill myself. I just wanted to feel better."

"Have you ever wanted to kill yourself?" she asked.

He nodded.

"Are you feeling that way now?"

Suddenly Clay realized that Dr. Williams's questions were not really designed to make him feel better. He wiped away the tears that had pooled in his eyes. Dr. Williams had already seen him cry once today. Once was enough.

"No," he said. He tried to make his voice sound strong and masculine.

"Are you sure?" she asked.

"I'm sure," he said. "I put the cutting behind me a long time ago, and I put those thoughts behind me when Noahleen got sick. I can't afford to kill myself now."

"What do you mean?"

"I can't kill myself. Noahleen doesn't have anyone else to take care of her, so I can't kill myself."

"Is that the only reason that you don't want to die?"

The world stopped around Clay, and for a moment, Dr. Williams looked like she was trapped. Stalled in mid-facial expression. Then the sound of the air conditioning vent above them filled Clay's ears and everything became brighter. He knew then that the answer was "yes," but that it did not have to be. Dr. Williams might not know what the university should do for him, but she had led him to a more important truth.

Before he could ask anyone else to give him what he wanted, he had to want something. Avoiding pain was not enough.

Somehow, during the years that he had been trying to act as the breadwinner for their household, he had forgotten the things he had wanted when Noahleen was still working. He had forgotten that there were goals that were bigger than being able to pay next month's rent without having to put her medication copays on a credit card.

"Clay, I need you to answer me," Dr. Williams said. "Would you kill yourself if you didn't have Noahleen?"

"No," he said. He meant it this time. "No. I don't want to be dead. I just want to be able to live without having dreams about how much better my life was when I would cut my arms open with razors. I need those dreams to stop, and I need to have enough space around me to be able to work without feeling like work is the only thing I do."

"I'm not sure I can help with that," she said. "Not in the sense of getting the university to lighten your class load, anyway. They pay you by the class, and I know you don't want to lose any income."

He nodded.

"So the question becomes, what can I do?"

Clay shrugged. "Get me an office? Someplace where I can close the door and be alone without having to worry about someone wanting me to leave so that they can use the space. Someplace where I don't have to use headphones, where I can just calm down completely on my own all the time. And I want after-hours access, too. I need to use it on the weekends and at night."

"You're not planning on living there, are you?"

He shook his head. "No, but I need a place I can retreat to. At home, I have an office, but I need a place I can leave my work. I need work and home to become separate things. And I need a place where I can go without having people follow me. A place where they won't be able to pen me in and make me do what they say."

Dr. Williams nodded. "I can't make any promises, but I will see what I can do."

Clay felt her eyes searching his face. He wanted to turn away from her, but he was afraid that she would take it the wrong way if he did.

"I'll do everything I can to help you," she said. "But there is one problem that we have to deal with before I can let you go."

"What?" Clay asked. "What else do you want from me?"

"I watched you hurt yourself, Clay. I watched you do something that made you a danger to yourself. We have to deal with that before I can let you go."

Clay felt his anger surge again, but he held his broken hand by the wrist with his good hand so that he could not lash out.

"What do you mean?" he asked. "We just dealt with it."

"No, Clay. We dealt with the workplace accommodations. I still can't let you leave until I'm sure you're not going to be a danger to yourself or others."

Clay held on to his broken hand, his right hand, by the wrist. He could feel it spasm from the elbow on down. If he let go of himself, he knew that he would wind up punching the wall again, and if he did that, then he could already feel that he would be throwing himself on the floor and banging his head against things. There was a familiar tension in his joints that told him so.

Instead, he forced himself to look Dr. Jeannie Williams in the eye. It made his entire body hurt to do it, but it also drained the fury out of his joints and let him shoot it at her through his pupils.

She looked away before he did.

He wanted nothing more than to stand up and smash her face in, but he knew that there would be no point to it. She could threaten to detain or imprison him with impunity as long as he had the broken hand, and any force that he used to resist her would only be turned into another excuse to hold him. He could not give in to it. He knew he could not give in to it.

The walls of the cubicle faded away and Clay felt himself falling into the past. He was running down the stairs of his childhood home, trying to make the front door before his mother caught him. She had been yelling at him from the kitchen even though he had his bedroom door closed, accusing him of hiding her medications. Accusing him of doing nothing but masturbating and stealing her cigarettes. He had never even smoked a cigarette, he was only in sixth grade.

He stumbled on the stairs and caught himself on the wrought-iron railing, but the noise brought his mother out from the kitchen. She saw him lunge for the doorknob and shouted: "Don't you dare go out that door!"

Clay tried to pull at the doorknob anyway, but her words were like a magic spell keeping his hands from obeying his will. He had no idea why he was incapable of disobeying her, and he kicked and threw himself against the inside of his own skull. The headache it produced was fantastic, but the panic that he felt from trying to disobey his mother's direct order made it hard for him to breathe.

She was getting closer. He did not want her to touch him, but he could not go out through the front door.

Clay pivoted and ran up the stairs, back toward his room. He heard her footsteps behind him, and part of him wanted to laugh because she still tried to stop him from watching horror movies, but she was always chasing him through the house and trying to hurt him in ways that felt just like those movies.

Somewhere, the adult that was remembering this let his mother's face be replaced by a hockey mask. It made the memory easier.

Sixth-grade Clay slammed the door behind him, but there was no lock, and even if there had been, he would not have time to turn it. She was just on his heels, and slamming the door in her face was only going to buy him time if he kept moving.

Without stopping, he realized that his bed, the place where he read his books and curled under blankets when he was afraid, was not going to be safe. It was in a corner, and his mother was about to come through the only door. He had two windows, though. One opened onto the roof of their back porch. He could jump through it and then run across the roof, jumping into the neighbor's tree. The other opened onto a thirty foot drop to the concrete patio below. Both were open, with only screens between himself and freedom.

He did not tell himself he was making a choice, he just ran. As his head cleared the screen, knocking the entire storm window off its frame, he suddenly felt fear. Something in him did not want to do this anymore, but the thirty foot drop was open beneath him. It was too late to change. Once he realized that the choice had already been made, the fear stopped and something else took its place. A vision of himself in bandages, or even a coffin.

His heart tightened in his chest, but then a warm feeling spread throughout his limbs. He might not be able to live anymore, but he could still win. Even if he didn't make it, even if he hit the concrete head first, the world would finally know what she did, and his father would not be able to blame it on his behavior.

As his body became weightless, clearing the window entirely, Clay realized that the warm and relaxed feeling that had overtaken him was hope. He spread his arms out to embrace the cement beneath him.

Then something caught his ankles. His face slammed into the aluminum siding instead of the concrete, and he could feel himself being hauled backward, back into the window. Back to her.

"How dare you?" She bellowed, and her screams seemed to give her strength. That was nothing new, though. His mother was like Lou Ferrigno's Hulk; she only became strong and monstrous after she started screaming.

He went limp and allowed her to pull him back into his room and away from freedom. Once she had him back inside, she shook him by the shoulders and screamed into his face. His body responded, trying to push away from her. He wished it would not do that. He knew it would only make her worse.

"What did you think you were doing?" she asked.

"Not going out the front door," he mumbled.

She hugged him hard. He screamed. Then it was all screaming in his head, and he could not remember what happened next.

Dr. Jeannie Williams was trying to do that now. She was trying to order him away from the door, and he had to think that she knew exactly what she was doing. That made her more of a monster and unlike his mother, he had no sense of guilt about the possibility of hurting her.

Clay stood up. Dr. Williams seemed to shrink against her chair.

"That was a mistake," Clay said. "Threatening to imprison me."

She stammered, but she did not make words. He wondered what his face looked like. Dr. Williams had never lost her words around him before.

He kind of liked knowing he could do that to her, but he stomped down that satisfaction because he knew that if he allowed it to take hold, then it would lead him into the place that he went when

Noahleen wanted to play games, and he knew that he should not go there with Dr. Williams. Dr. Williams was not playing games.

"I am going to leave now, and you are going to disclose to the university that we had a previous relationship. You have about fifteen minutes to tell someone, because I'm going straight to Human Resources to file a complaint. I'm telling them that the clinical psychologist they contracted to evaluate me is someone I had already severed a relationship with because she did not want to treat me. I'll tell them you threatened to institutionalize me if I did not consent to the prescription of strong and dangerous tranquilizers."

He leaned into her personal space. She flinched, but he made sure that only his face got close to her.

"I'm not going to call any local medical associations or contact a lawyer yet. You're going to accept my side of the story and apologize, and then the university will never ask you to consult again, because of this lapse in your professional ethics. If you don't let that happen, then I will call a lawyer. It doesn't matter if the only lawyer I can afford is an ambulance chaser—in fact, an ambulance chaser might be better, because I won't be doing it for money. I will be doing it to fill your life with unproductive bullshit and demands that don't make sense. Do you understand why?"

She did not move. He backed away from her.

"Do you understand why I would rather take all of your attention, time, and personal resources instead of taking your money? Do you understand what it would make you, if every day you had to spend your entire day thinking about what someone might randomly do to create unnecessary obstacles for you, or to make you conform to stupid meeting schedules that won't change anything or lead to any solutions?"

She nodded. Just once. Just a little. Still, she nodded.

"Good," Clay said. "Now, I am going to do what I should have done in the first place. I am going to go. Don't even think about trying to play games with me, because my first accusation is going to be that you only accepted this consultation to pursue a relationship with me after your harassment led me to abandon my only access to any form of medical or psychological care. If you claim I'm suicidal, I'm going to claim that I became that way when the university forced me to be alone with a doctor who abused me. Are we clear?"

She nodded again. Suddenly, Dr. Williams seemed very small.

He turned and walked out of the cubicle. No one stopped him. No one stopped him from going out the front door of the university's counseling center either.

When the fresh air hit him, though, he felt like he was crumpling in on himself. Whatever momentary confidence he had gained after he flashed back to that memory of his mother was deflating, and he could feel it getting harder to walk. Still, he made it to the administration building and up the three flights of stairs to Human Resources.

As he stood in the doorway and looked around to see if there was a receptionist or someone else that he should talk to first, a dizzy feeling like a headrush surged up his spine and into his brain. The office in front of him dissolved into black and green flecks then, and even though he tried to hold on to the door frame, he still felt himself toppling forward.

He never felt the tile floor hit his forehead. By then, he was not feeling anything except the knotty tension in his joints that let him know that he was about to lose control over his entire body for an unpredictable amount of time.

❖ ❖ ❖

The Slow Turn Out of a Nose Dive

Clay opened his eyes to a ceiling that looked suspiciously like his old dorm room ceiling. After a few fuzzy moments, it occurred to him that this meant that he was still at the university. He remembered making it up the stairs to Human Resources, but then everything was foggy. Had he collapsed? If so, then where was he?

It was dim in the room. No lights were on, and the blinds on the sole window were closed. Clay was lying on a couch, so it could not be his office. It was definitely a university office like his, though. It was just bigger.

He sat up and looked around.

Once he was properly oriented to the room, he was able to navigate the layout of the couches, the coffee machine, and the cheap fake ficus plant. Someone had moved him to a lounge and closed the door. Was he still in Human Resources?

He went to the door and opened it. When he did, he saw that Dr. Brown was there, talking to a man in scrubs and a woman in a nice suit. All three of them stopped and smiled at Clay when they noticed him.

"Am I interrupting something?" Clay asked.

"No," Dr. Brown said. "We were actually just waiting for you to wake up. Let's go back inside and talk." He gestured toward the lounge.

"Am I still in Human Resources?" Clay asked as he turned around.

"Yes, you are," the woman replied. "We didn't want to move you too far."

Clay nodded as he led them back into the room. He sat himself on one of the couches and waited. One of the other people turned on the light, which made him flinch. He heard himself make a hissing noise and cursed his stupid voice for making noises without permission. After a few seconds, the light got more tolerable, but he could already hear the hum in the lightbulbs. This was going to be a trial.

"So first of all," Dr. Brown said, "we did have to call a nurse over from the university's clinic to check you out. He said that you weren't injured from the fall, at least as much as he could tell. Does your head hurt? Or anything else?"

Clay shook his head. "I could really use the lights being turned off, though."

He felt the room around him pause. Dr. Brown looked to the nurse, who furrowed his brow.

"I don't have a fucking concussion, I'm autistic! Just turn the lights off," Clay said. When they did, he apologized for cursing.

"Are you hypoglycemic? Have you ever had a history of fainting?" The nurse did not wait for further introductions.

"No," Clay said, "and I don't want you poking at me. I feel fine. Or at least as fine as I usually do after something like this."

"Okay," the nurse said, "I'm just going to do a couple of tests. Can you follow my finger with your eyes?" He held up one finger in front of Clay's face.

"I can, but I don't want to," Clay said.

"Clay," Dr. Brown's voice was flat. "We're going to need you to comply with some tests. This counts as a workplace accident, which means we can't let you go back to work without checking you out."

Clay scoffed.

"I'm serious. You need to either comply with the nurse or you need to go home and see your own doctor. Either way, we're not able to let you stay until you're checked out. It's a liability issue."

"Fine," Clay said. "Are you going to make me piss in a cup too? To make sure I'm not getting high before I do dangerous things like contact Human Resources about a workplace conflict?"

Dr. Brown looked at the nurse. The nurse shook his head. "Not necessary this time," he said.

"No," Dr. Brown said. "But were you?"

When Dr. Brown asked his question, the woman in the suit cleared her throat.

"Never mind," Dr. Brown said. "Just let the nurse check you out. The university's paying for it, and if he finds something that forces us to send you to the emergency room, then the university will pay for that too."

Clay felt himself perking up when Dr. Brown mentioned the university paying for his health care. For a second, he wondered why it had never occurred to him to get hurt at work before. Then he felt ashamed of himself and a little disgusted.

"I don't do well with doctors," he said out loud. "It's been years since one of them touched me."

He stared at Dr. Brown when he said this. Dr. Brown gave him a knowing nod.

"Well," the nurse said, "it's a good thing I'm not a doctor."

The woman in the suit chuckled with him at his joke. Dr. Brown and Clay just stared at each other.

Clay nodded to Dr. Brown, and then he turned his attention to the nurse. For a few minutes, the nurse asked him to do various things—following a finger with his eyes, squeezing his fingers, standing and walking... then something fell into place in Clay's mind.

"Are you checking to see if I've had a seizure?" he asked.

"Actually, yes," the nurse replied. "Whenever there's a collapse, we're supposed to check for concussion, fever, seizure, and blood sugar. Did you want me to check your blood sugar? I have test strips, but I usually don't push them on patients unless they have a history of problems with that."

Clay shook his head. "I'm not post-ictal," he said. "My wife's epileptic. I know what that would be like."

"I'm sure you do," the nurse said, "but you don't know what it would feel like. We're almost done."

Clay grunted, but he complied with the nurse's next few requests. After the man was done, he pronounced that Clay was fine and left the room.

"Well," Dr. Brown started, "what the hell happened today?"

The woman in the suit leaned forward and started talking before Clay could respond.

"Mr. Dillon? Is it okay if I call you Clay?"

Clay nodded.

"Good. Clay, I think you were on your way to talk to me, and the reason I think this is because just after you collapsed, I received a phone call notifying me that Dr. Jeannie Williams has resigned as a consultant at the university's counseling center. She did not give a reason, except to say that she has decided to focus on her private practice. She did give instructions to us to accommodate you as reasonably as we could, but to be aware that your position is already uniquely suited to your needs in a lot of ways."

Clay nodded.

"Is there anything else you wanted to tell us? Anything that happened that made you so upset?"

Clay nodded. The woman waited for a few seconds, but when Clay did not say anything, she frowned at him.

"Is something wrong?"

Clay tried to say "no," but he could not make himself talk. Instead, he held up a hand and shook his head.

Dr. Brown leaned in. "I think he might still be upset by whatever happened." To Clay, he said, "We can leave you alone for a few minutes if you want."

Clay shook his head. He tried to talk again, but he just wound up waving his hands. Finally, he opened his mouth and took a few great, sucking breaths that made him feel like his chest had been hollowed out. Suddenly, he found himself able to speak again.

"I had been seeing Dr. Williams, but I separated from her when I became uncomfortable with her professional recommendations. She told me point-blank that she would not help me to access services and that I should not disclose at work. When I questioned this or any other therapeutic advice, she became pushy. Today, she threatened to have me held for a psychiatric observation. It was all I could do to get out of there."

As the words came out, he knew that they were not a lie but that they were also not all of what happened. He hoped that the lady in the suit did not have too many questions, because he was not sure that he could make very many more words.

The woman in the suit did not say anything for a few seconds. Her eyes were wide.

Dr. Brown fidgeted in his chair.

Clay waited.

"That is… shocking," the woman finally said. "We really didn't anticipate that. I'm sorry."

Dr. Brown nodded.

"Look," the woman in the suit said, "we do want to work with you, but I'm going to be honest—we've never had to accommodate anything other than sight, hearing, and mobility issues before. I don't know what to do for you, and unless you ask for specific accommodations, the only thing I can do is ask a psychologist or an occupational therapist for advice. Either of those kinds of people will want to meet you. So we seem to be at an impasse."

Clay nodded.

"Do you remember what I told you when I observed your classroom?" Dr. Brown asked.

Clay nodded.

"You need to do that now. You need to go home and talk to whoever you have for support, and you need to come back with a clear plan that tells us what you need. Otherwise, we can't help you."

Clay nodded again. He did not know what else to do.

"We will wait for you to submit a request for accommodations," the woman said. Then she stood up and left the room.

"Come on, Clay. I'll give you a ride home," Dr. Brown said.

"I have a car," Clay replied.

"If you want, I'll have someone drive it home for you. I don't think it's a good idea for you to drive right now," Dr. Brown replied. "Let's go."

Clay thought about resisting, but it was too much effort. He dug his keys out of his pocket and handed them to Dr. Brown.

"Drive me in my car, please," he said.

Dr. Brown nodded and led him out of the room, then out of the building. Neither of them said anything on the drive home, but Clay thought that Dr. Brown looked like he wanted to talk. There would be time for that later. For now, it was just too much for Clay to think about. He needed to conserve his strength for Noahleen, who would want to know what had happened and why he had not driven himself home.

Just thinking about what to tell her made his joints knot up, and Clay had to take several deep breaths to avoid punching the ceiling in the car. When they arrived at his apartment, Dr. Brown took the keys out of the ignition and handed them to Clay.

"Do you need to use the phone? To call for a ride back to campus?"

Clay asked.

Dr. Brown shook his head. "Thank you, though. I think I'm going to walk back. I need to clear my head."

"It's a long way," Clay said.

"I know," Dr. Brown replied, "but it's a nice day, and I need some time to think."

Clay watched his department head walk away from the building. As Dr. Brown moved across the apartment complex, he stared at the buildings around himself as if they might come to life and try to eat him. For a moment, Clay worried about him, but then his mind returned to Noahleen. He had barely spoken to her about his problems since the night when he had broken his hand. She blamed herself for that—Clay could tell—and he knew that his silence was not helping her. At the same time, though, he felt like he could not start a conversation with her because he was too ashamed of himself, so every time they talked, it was just about television or what to have for dinner.

There was the sex, though. That was still good, but it only happened in the middle of the night and neither of them talked about it afterward. It was violent, and it was a relief, but it worried him that it only seemed to happen when one or the other of them woke up in the dark.

❖ ❖ ❖

Demanding Change

Clay had not told Noahleen about Dr. Jeannie Williams being the psychologist that the university assigned to do his evaluation. He had intended to do it, but when the moment of truth came, he realized that he did not want to have to explain why he had initially separated from her, since he had been pretending that his therapy was going well for several weeks after ending it. Knowing that he was hiding so much from Noahleen made him anxious, which made it harder for him to be around her, but the idea of telling her was terrifying.

Instead, he told her that he had finally had a panic attack in full view, and that Dr. Brown had insisted that he take the rest of the day off after seeing how drastic his symptoms were. Noahleen nodded her understanding about that and, thankfully, left him alone afterward.

For the rest of that afternoon, Clay sat around the living room. He spent a lot of time reading, because reading was a way for him to think deeply and to experience the lives of others without taxing himself. He did not try to go to the office, though, because he knew that once he was alone with his work papers, he would feel compelled to work.

Staying in the apartment's common areas for once not only allowed him to remain separate from his work, it also forced him to see the way that Noahleen moved through her daily tasks. Over the past few months, Clay had mostly avoided spending time around her unless they were watching television together or helping each other with chores. He did not tell himself that it was because his diagnosis and his dreams about being able to pass for either male or female were making him afraid, but in the foggy, not-verbal part of his brain where everything was an image and memories ran together into collages, he knew it was true.

The part of his brain that did make words and announce his decisions to himself knew that this behavior was unfair, but it was not strong enough to suggest a way of remedying the situation to the rest of him. As he watched Noahleen move through her chores, though, his guilt mounted. She worked hard to keep the house in order, but even so, the "house" was barely five hundred square feet, and after a very short time, she had nothing left to do.

For a while, she joined Clay on the couch to re-read *American Gods*, but he could see from the way that the book's spine collapsed and its ragged pages folded in on themselves that she had read the book so much it was worn out. After she finished reading, she closed it and stared at the television's empty screen for several minutes.

"I need something to do," she said. "I know you don't know what that should be, but if I don't have a project of my own, I will eventually start drinking just to pass the time. Neither one of us wants that. Not with the kind of medication I'm already taking."

Clay nodded.

"The problem is that the bus line around here sucks. I have to ride for a half hour just to get to the exchange, and then I have to take at least one more bus to get anywhere in town. The route we're on only goes to other apartment buildings."

Clay nodded again.

"I'm only even saying this out loud because I need you to know why I'm always unhappy. I need you to realize, too, that ignoring me is only making my life more empty. I can't take it any more. Either you come home and speak, or you find me a job that doesn't care if I have to call in sick five or six times every month. I don't care what it is. I'm not screwing around on the internet all day and calling that a life. There's only so much Farmville that a mind can take."

After that, she got up from the couch and left the apartment. Clay was thankful, because he really did not know how to respond to her, and he knew that if she stayed, she would be expecting him to talk.

❖ ❖ ❖

It was dark, but Clay could see the outline of his own face because the dim glow of the LED nightlight was just strong enough to illuminate the boundaries of objects. It was not strong enough to show him his own facial expression, but he felt like he would not want that anyway.

Briefly, he wondered how he had come to be in the bathroom. He could tell by the smell and the echoes of his own breathing that that was where he was. Well, from those things and from the fact that he could see himself in a mirror. He did not recall waking up and walking into the room, though. His first memory of being there was when the sound of his razor falling onto the ground startled him.

Sleepwalking was new. Kind of. It had happened once or twice when he was much younger, but he could not recall it being an issue for more than a decade. Still, here he was. In the bathroom, watching himself in the mirror.

He had been holding the razor before he woke up.

Was this because of Noahleen? Was he feeling guilty about hiding so much of himself from her?

Or perhaps it was because he had been so wrapped up in himself that he had completely ignored her need for support for several months now?

Earlier, when he had reached out for her in the dark, she had removed his hand from her body and wrapped herself in her own blanket. That was unusual, even for their recent distance. Usually, she responded to his touch no matter what. Their relationship had always been driven by that.

Clay tried to shrug off the disappointment and to focus on what the change in her behavior really meant, but it was hard to ignore the pangs of thwarted desire without ignoring the entire situation. Maybe this was something that he needed to be fully awake to deal with.

He turned to walk himself back to the bedroom and slammed his face into a closed door instead. Staggering, he stepped back, only to stumble into the sink and hurt his hip. How had he closed the door in his sleep?

For that matter, how had he managed to take the razor out of his shaving kit? That kit was locked up in the medicine cabinet.

Using his hands to map his position by feeling the walls and fixtures, Clay eased himself down onto the toilet seat. He needed to get a firm grip on his spatial orientation before he tried to go back to the bedroom. If he did not, he might wind up really hurting himself.

He forced himself to take deep, slow breaths and to ignore the stinging spots on his face and hip where he had just collided with his environment. Dwelling on those things would only make him feel embarrassed, and since no one was there to see him crashing around, embarrassment was unproductive.

While he was doing his breathing and wondering how long it would take before his heart rate went back down to normal, the bathroom door opened and light washed over him, forcing him to close his eyes. He heard himself shout, but it was more like a shriek.

"What the hell?"

Noahleen's voice.

Clay blinked tears out of his eyes and tried to look at her, but she had turned all the lights on—both the bathroom lights and the hallway lights. When he tried to open his eyes, the light hurt, so he squinted at her and tried not to cry.

She was naked and angry, which surprised him, because usually she was not angry when he got out of bed in the middle of the night. Usually, she ignored him. At most, she asked questions when he got back into bed. Not this time. This time, her shoulders were shaking and she kept stomping her feet.

"What the fuck is wrong with you? And how long have you been doing this?"

Clay shook his head. What was she talking about?

"Enough, Clay! I know you don't like to talk when you're upset, but this is it. I need to know why you are hiding from me, and I need to know what all this means."

He tried to open his eyes again, but the light hurt. Keeping the squint going so that he could see her face, he shrugged.

"I can't see," he said. "I can't see what you're upset about. I just woke up in here and then I hurt myself when I tried to leave the room because I didn't know the door was closed."

She stopped shaking and stepped in front of him. He looked at her hands, because they were reaching out for him. When they brushed his neck, pain flared. Each place a finger landed lit up.

"What have you been doing here?" she asked.

He could feel that his neck was hurt, but he did not know what she was talking about. He said as much.

"You didn't do this?" she asked. "Then who did?"

He shrugged.

"I still don't know what this is," he said.

Her hands ran down his chest. In a few spots, they spread something wet across his body. He felt a twitch in his genitals when that happened, but he tried to suppress it.

"You need to look," she said. "Look at yourself. I mean it."

She held her arm out to him. He took it and let her help him stand. Still squinting, he managed, with Noahleen's help, to turn and face the mirror. Even with his reduced field of vision, he could see that he looked battered. There were bruises on his chest that looked greenish-yellow, like they had been fading for a while. Red welts ran down the sides of his neck in trails. They were probably from fingernails. A row of cuts between his sternum and his belly button oozed blood slowly. They were partially scabbed over.

He shut his eyes against it all.

"I don't know," he said. "I don't know what happened."

"You did this," Noahleen said. "Maybe you did it in your sleep, but you did this. I've been in bed all night. I woke a little when you got up, but then I fell asleep again until I heard you crashing around. How could you do this?"

"I literally don't know," Clay said. "I just woke up."

"Some of these injuries are old. At least a few days old, maybe older," Noahleen said. "Tell me the truth. How long have you been doing this?"

"I told you," Clay said. "I don't know."

He could feel his adrenaline surging. Noahleen was calling him a liar, and he could not handle that right now. He had to worry about why his sleepwalking mind was trying to hurt him. The ragged lines of injury looked like something from a horror movie, like the injuries that victims left on the slasher killer when they tried to fight him off.

Suddenly he felt very tired.

"I want to sit down again," he said.

When he tried to go back to the toilet, Noahleen seized hold of his arm and led him out of the room instead. He tried to protest, but she ignored him and guided him to the couch in the living room. He sat.

"I can't do this," she said.

He nodded.

"No, I mean it," she continued, "I have been trying not to bother you because I know that you are having trouble. I know that work and diagnosis and therapy and all of that is a lot to balance. I've wanted you to have your space. I can't do that any longer, though. I can't let you ignore me while you tear yourself apart. And I don't believe you when you pretend that you don't know why you're so upset. I believe that maybe you were sleepwalking when you hurt yourself, but I don't believe that you're clueless about why you're sleepwalking.

"You're going to tell me what you did. What you're keeping from me. If you don't, then I'm going to stay with my parents until you decide to treat me like a partner and not a room mate who is constantly underfoot."

He nodded. Then he kept nodding. It was like he was locked into the motion, and the longer he did it, the harder and faster he needed to go. Noahleen did not try to stop him, but she did not leave him alone either.

After his nodding had evolved into full-body rocking, words started to fall out of his mouth. He told her then about his separation from Dr. Williams. He also confessed that the doctor had dismissed the idea that he was really disabled and that she had told him that she would never do any disability paperwork to support him. Finally, he told her about passing out in Human Resources. He did not mention that the university had required him to be evaluated by Dr. Williams. Clay was not sure why he held this back, but he found himself doing it anyway.

Noahleen stood in front of him the whole time. She took all his words in, letting her skin prickle up into a wall of goosebumps as he talked. She did not even move to grab a blanket from the edge of the couch. She just endured.

Clay knew then that he had made a terrible mistake when he had decided to hide things from her. Noahleen was stronger than he was, and he had not been able to see that. She might not be able to support them any longer, but she was still strong, and she had always been willing to stand between him and the world. He had been a fool to ignore that.

He felt himself crying long before he knew what was happening.

"It's not your fault I broke my hand," he said. "I don't think it's my fault either, but I think I've been acting like it's your fault when it's just something that happened."

He felt her stand closer to him. Her knees brushed against his, and then she was standing between his legs. He leaned forward and held her. He could feel her hands resting on the top and back of his head as she pulled him closer.

His broken hand cracked in several places.

"Yuck," she said, giggling through her disgust.

"Sorry," he said.

"Don't be," she replied. "Just don't... don't do this any more. I can't think of what else to say. You might be earning for us, but you're not running this show on your own. Don't sneak around on me. It never works out for either of us."

He nodded. She hugged him tighter. His body felt her skin against his cheek, under his hands, against his thighs. It did what it always did, and this time Clay did not try to stop himself. He kissed Noahleen's belly. Deeply. His lips trailed up her torso, finding her breasts, bringing them to his tongue and his tongue to them.

He heard Noahleen gasp, but then he felt her disappear. All of her except her hands, which rested on his shoulders.

"Not now," she said. "No."

"But..." he could not think of a sentence to follow that word.

"I can't," she said. "Not like this. Not while I'm still thinking about... everything."

He nodded. His heart sank.

"Is there anything else you're hiding from me?" she asked. "Really. I need to know."

He felt himself nodding again.

"Something about the therapist again?"

He shook his head no. He did not have the words to talk about his body feelings, about his regrets, but he had to let her know that there was still something there.

"I can't deal with you hiding things any more," she said.

"I'm not trying to," he replied. "I just don't know that I have words for all of it."

She did not say anything then.

"I will tell you before I tell anyone," he said. "But I can't find words. I just... I'm embarrassed and it hurts a lot."

Her hands left his shoulders.

"I'm going to go lay down," she said. "When you come back to bed, wake me up and tell me. I'm not going anywhere, but I don't want you to touch me until you tell me what is bothering you so much."

He listened to her moving around the apartment until she turned all the lights back off and closed all the doors. Then he let himself lay down on the couch. Instead of sleeping, he used his hands to trace his body in the dark. He sought out all the parts that hurt, teasing them one by one. As each one screamed, he felt himself getting more and more aroused.

When he started to masturbate, he kept one hand on his chest. He tried to imagine what it would be like, if the muscle that ran under his skin was soft. If it was as soft as Noahleen's skin. He fell asleep before he finished, and in his dreams, he felt his own breasts pushing against hers. There was no chest hair to come between them, and she giggled at him while she kissed his neck.

In the morning, he found fresh scratches on his chest, running from his clavicle diagonally to his flank. He hated that he now had another injury to explain to Noahleen, but he was starting to feel like he might have an explanation.

❖ ❖ ❖

Falling Back Into The Routine

The days after Clay's midnight confrontation with Noahleen were a little blurry for him. He knew that he was making his schedule work and that he was attending all the classes that he was supposed to teach, but every night, as he lay in bed, he would mentally tally the tasks he had accomplished during the day. Often, he found himself unable to name them. He felt tired.

All the time, he felt tired. He knew that he was spending a lot of time on the couch when he was not grading or teaching, but the actual passage of hours eluded Clay. Instead, his day was a fractured mosaic of sensory impressions and half-forgotten conversations with people whose concerns seemed banal for reasons that Clay could not articulate.

Through the haze, Clay caught himself having thoughts about removing his body hair and dieting back down to one hundred and eighty pounds. When he was on Facebook, he often found himself looking back at pictures from when he was in college, when he was thin and beardless and very often indistinguishable from the women he was hugging in the photographs. He had not told himself that he was trying to look like them back when he was doing it, but it was obvious now. Even his clothing was like theirs. He did not wear dress shirts or polos, he wore Oxford tops and flare-legged khakis.

Noahleen often checked on him while he was floating around in his haze. He was glad for that. As long as he answered her questions, she gave him peace. Still, when he reached out for her, she was not available for anything more than a hug. He understood that this was the new way between them, but he missed the old way, and his more collected moments were spent trying to figure out how to talk to her, to rebuild their connection.

Through it all, he was aware of giving her vague answers to questions about Dr. Williams and about the university. Mostly, though, he just felt like he was falling into the couch.

He slept a lot, too. His body seemed to be taking revenge on him by mixing up sleepwalking with this kind of semi-conscious waking state where he could not make himself complete a train of thought. He wondered what he would do if there was suddenly a need for him to push himself. If, say, Noahleen started having seizures again.

Then she did.

They were not very bad, at least at first, but the fact that Clay was feeling so lethargic was very bad, because when Noahleen started to seize, he did not realize it. Not until her knees were sagging and she was starting to tip to one side. Clay jumped off the couch when he saw that, but by the time he was in the kitchen and able to reach out for her, she was already falling. The result was that he lurched forward to grab her as her head hit the wall, and he nearly fell on top of her when her weight dragged him down.

Clay maintained his balance—barely—but the most he could do for Noahleen was to ease her fall. Once she was safely lying on the kitchen floor, he had to watch and wait.

That was the worst part, the watching.

He knew from experience that basically any intervention was the wrong intervention, but he still had to repeat it to himself. It was hard to see her there, on the floor, twitching and slowly turning her body over, but if he tried to hold her or stop her, she would either injure him or herself. He did not dare to look away or walk away, though, because if she turned herself too much, there was the possibility that she could block her own airway. That had happened once, and it was only luck that she had been found before she suffocated.

Eventually, Noahleen became still. Clay looked at the clock. It seemed like he had been watching her for hours, but he saw that it was actually only three minutes.

He kept watching.

It was another minute or two before she yawned and sat up, indicating that she felt stable enough to stand with help. The yawn was good, and it made Clay feel good. It made him feel like she had just been moving in her sleep, the way that he did sometimes. He knew better, but in the moment, when her weight was pulling at him and he was guiding her to the couch as she staggered around, it made him feel good.

"I'm getting the migraine," she said. "You need to cook dinner tonight."

Clay nodded. The fog that he had been living in for several days was gone already, and he knew he could do what he needed to do for Noahleen.

"Get my lorazepam," she said. "I don't want to go to the hospital until we've tried to fix this ourselves."

Clay went to the medicine cabinet and retrieved two pills. Each was a full milligram of lorazepam. The bottle said that she should only take one, but he was going to give her two. Just in case. She had taken up to five before, so he knew that it was safe to give her two, and he wanted to make sure that they did not have to fight escalating seizures all night. It would be better if she just started with two.

When he returned to Noahleen and handed her the pills, she nodded at him. Two was a good choice. He knew. He always second-guessed his judgment, but she knew. Whatever he gave her, she never second-guessed him.

After she took the pills, Noahleen agreed to lay down on the couch so that he could go into the kitchen and cook dinner without having to worry about her falling over again.

Clay knew what to do. He knew how to handle Noahleen's problem and how long she would need to come back to herself, to be ready to get off the couch and do her daily routine again. The only hard part was going to be class time. Clay could work from home for most of the day, but class time was time he had to leave, and he always hated doing that while Noahleen was sick.

Noahleen managed to remain seizure free for most of the night, and the couple watched television together and laughed at the narcissism of the contestants on Hell's Kitchen. It was just like normal, except that Noahleen needed an arm whenever she wanted to stand up, and Clay needed to wait on her because he did not want her to try to pour her own soda or serve herself food if she needed a stabilizing arm just to walk to the bathroom.

Part of him knew that this meant that things were actually completely normal, not normal "except" for those things. He knew he should embrace that part of himself that knew these things, but it was a frightening aspect, and he tried instead to ignore it.

Instead, he thought about how much sex they'd have after she recovered. She always craved physical contact after the pain and confusion from the seizures retreated. It might be several weeks, but Clay knew that it would happen, that her feeling healthy again would be all it took for them to put this strange distance behind themselves.

He still had to worry about teaching his classes without leaving her alone for too long, though. In the meantime.

❖ ❖ ❖

Picking Up The Pieces

Clay tried not to yell at Noahleen, but every cell of his being was screaming at him that he was uncomfortable and it was her fault. He squashed his impulses, though, and squirmed in his seat instead of speaking. It would not be fair to yell at her. She was just trying to read, and she was letting him grade his papers. He was the one who had insisted on bringing her to work, and they would be going home just as soon as his mandatory hour in the office was over. At least he did not have any students coming in for conferences this week.

He wished he could stop arguing with himself. It was distracting, and it kept him from getting his work done.

Of course, he would not have to argue with himself if Noahleen was not there, giggling into the pages of *American Gods* for the who-knows-how-many-third time.

Of course, leaving her at home would mean leaving her without any assistance if she started seizing again, and in a third floor apartment to boot.

Clay felt himself grinding his teeth.

The first couple of days after she started seizing had been terrible. Clay had been forced to spend an entire weekend coaxing her back to health, dosing her regularly on as many lorazepam as he felt she could safely tolerate. Even keeping her mostly unconscious and keeping the apartment dim and quiet had not helped, though. Every twenty minutes for a full twenty-four hours, she had drifted into a fugue, only to emerge after the seizure. It always started by contorting her face as her smile pulled into a rictus on one side (and only one side). From there, it traveled down her body and through her hands and feet before spending itself.

Each time her movement petered out and she returned to sleep, Clay contemplated the confusing and sometimes dangerous movements that traveled through her. They looked almost like an orgasm that happened slowly and with more violence, and that took hold of only half of her. When he allowed himself to think of the seizure in those terms, though, it made him queasy. Still, he made himself confront his impressions.

On the third day of seizure activity, the rescue medication slowly started to work. Instead of an episode every twenty minutes, Noahleen only had a couple of bad hours, one in the morning before she took her meds and another in the afternoon during the lead-up to her next dose. The hour before her bedtime medication was thankfully tranquil.

Today, though, was the fourth day. She had not seized since they had been awake, but Clay was not about to run the risk that she would start if he left her alone. He was also barely able to tolerate her constant presence when he was trying to stay focused on his routine, but he could hardly show her that. Instead, he forced himself to stop fidgeting and to ignore her, and he looked at the stack of quizzes he was supposed to be grading instead.

After he had finished three more, Noahleen yawned.

"How long before we can go home?" she asked. "I'm getting hungry."

Clay looked at his cell phone. He was actually past the end of his hour. He checked his stack of graded quizzes. He had managed to mark five of them during the hour. Normally, he would be finished with at least this one class by now. Inwardly, he sighed. At least if he went home, he would be able to go into his office and close the door.

"Come on," he said. "We can go now."

"Are you sure? I don't want you to get into trouble for leaving early," she said.

"No, we're actually a little over the end of my time. I need to leave before the next person comes in to use the office. There are several of us who have to share the space."

Noahleen nodded.

Clay gathered his things and then helped her into her jacket. When she stood up, she wobbled a little. He hoped it was just the legacy of her tranquilizers and not the beginning of a new wave of instability. Either way, he made sure to hold tightly onto her elbow as they worked their way down the hall to the elevators.

On their way out of the department, Dr. Brown saw them and waved. Clay waved back.

"Is he the one who is helping you get your accommodations?" Noahleen asked.

Clay hushed her. He did not know who was aware of his situation, and he did not want to discuss it openly when he had no idea who might overhear it.

Finally, the elevator came for them, and he was able to get Noahleen onto it. Once the doors were closed, he told her that he did not want to talk out loud about private things because there were so many people packed into offices that were so close together, and he knew the gossip would spread like wildfire. Before she could respond, though, the elevator doors opened again, and Clay took her elbow and steered her through the lobby and out of the building. Other than a couple of stumbles over some uneven pavement, the two of them made it to the car without incident. As Clay held the door for Noahleen, she told him that he should just relax and that she would be fine.

"We don't know that," he said as he closed the door.

During the ride home, she kept insisting that she knew the seizure episode was over, but Clay kept reminding her that every time he had relaxed his vigilance too early, they had wound up in the hospital because of injuries that she sustained during her seizures.

Neither of them wanted to go back to the hospital.

"You can't just hover over me all the time though," Noahleen said. "I mean, what about your appointment with your therapist? You usually do that after class on Tuesdays, and it's Tuesday. What are you going to do with me? If you leave me at home, then you're breaking your own rules and admitting that it would have been fine to leave me alone all day. If you bring me into the session, though, she's going to wonder why and it's going to be disruptive." She made a face at him. "I saw how disruptive it was for you when you were trying to grade, so don't pretend I'm wrong."

"Don't worry about my appointment," he said. "I'm not going to miss anything."

Noahleen did not let the topic drop. Instead, she kept asking what he was going to do. At first, Clay tried to deflect her, but when she started insisting that he not cancel his appointments because his health and his therapy was at least as important as her own, he finally broke down.

"Look, I'm not seeing the therapist any more," he said. "Okay? I quit. Before I even asked for accommodations at work, I quit her. She wasn't doing any good anyway. Look at me—look at my temper. Look at our relationship."

He thrust his fist into Noahleen's face.

"Look at my fucking hand. Whatever she was doing, it was enough to provoke me into escalating my meltdowns this much." He waved the hand at her. She flinched. "So I quit. I was more stable before I was diagnosed than I am right now, so whatever she wanted me to do, it was the wrong thing. I'm sorry I didn't tell you, but I didn't want you to think that I was giving up. I'm not giving up, I'm just trying to figure out something that works."

Noahleen did not say anything for a long time. Finally, she just asked him how his going untreated would affect his workplace accommodations.

Clay shrugged. He did not want to tell her about his final meeting with Dr. Williams. He could already feel her hurt and betrayal emanating from her after his other revelation. Still, he knew that it would probably be better to tell her now, while she was already dealing with having been deceived. If he waited, then she would just have to go through all of this again.

Even knowing that, though, he still found himself struggling to make words that would describe what happened. Instead, he just said, "I don't know. The university wanted to observe me before they suggested accommodations, but I don't think that they should be able to do that. They got insistent, though. They wanted to use Dr. Williams."

"Obviously that would be a disaster," Noahleen said.

Clay nodded. "Obviously."

"So what's going to happen now?" Noahleen asked.

"Now? I'm taking you home and putting you in front of the television, and then I am going into my office to finish my grading. I'll make you dinner when I'm done."

"You don't need to do that," Noahleen said. "I can make dinner."

"No," Clay replied. "Not right now. Get a few more days between yourself and the seizures. Then you can make me dinner."

Noahleen nodded. Then she turned to look out the window. For the rest of the car ride, she kept looking out the window on her side of the car, letting Clay drive. He was grateful to her for that, for letting him concentrate.

❖ ❖ ❖

Coming To Terms

Clay was done grading by the time Noahleen knocked on his office door. Normally, he would have been a little short with her for poking her head in when she knew he was going to be working, but not today. Today, he was still on seizure watch, and no communication from her was unimportant. It also helped that he was done with his work and that he had just been staring at a blank wall and letting his mind relax.

"Clay?" She asked as she poked her face around the edge of the door. "We need to talk."

Clay shrugged. "I'm done with my work," he said, "come on in and talk."

Noahleen nodded. Then the door swung open all the way, revealing her body. She stepped into the room like she was trying to cross a creek on stepping stones—each step involved reaching out and patiently testing the footing she found before putting her weight on it. Clay took a deep breath and told himself that he needed to be patient because he was the one who had made her hesitant to invade his space.

Once she was in the room, she half-sat on the edge of his desk.

"This needs to stop," Noahleen said.

"I need you to explain what you're talking about," Clay replied. "There are a lot of things going on right now, and I don't know where we're starting."

Noahleen gestured to the room around her. "All of it. I've had enough."

A lump like the beginning of a sore throat formed in Clay's

esophagus. When he tried to talk around it, he realized that it was terror, not a lump, and that it had managed to seize control of his vocal chords. Instead of talking, he just shook his head.

"I'm sick of being ignored until the middle of the night and then waking up to find you fucking on top of me. For a while it was exciting, but now it feels like you're doing it instead of having a relationship with me. It doesn't feel like part of who we are anymore. And I'm sick of not knowing where you're going and how you're dealing with everything. I know that coming to terms with what your diagnosis means about your life and your childhood is hard. I know that you're angry. That you're probably wondering whether or not your parents knew, and if they knew, why they ignored your situation. You probably feel like our entire life together has been caused by their failure to support you and to teach you the things you would need to know about yourself.

"You know what? You're right. Dead on. But I'm not your mother, and I'm not responsible for the years of missed signals and neglect. I tried to give you the space you needed to come to terms with yourself. Hell, I tried to let you stay at home and grow your business and generally just weird out. I didn't know you were autistic, but I knew you had your own way of doing things, and I just thought you would find success if you were given the chance to do everything your own way. I was almost right, too. It's not my fault that my brain got in our way, just like it's not your fault that you get so frustrated that you lose control over your limbs and you break things. I can't stop having seizures. You can't stop yourself from getting frustrated. That's just the way we are. Whether you know it or not, though, you act like these are things we should be able to control. And I'm sick of it. I'm sick of feeling guilty all the time for things I can't control, and I'm sick of watching you dash yourself to pieces against your own expectations. I'm sick of not talking, and I'm sick of watching you collapse on the couch every night when you can't take the work any more. I've had enough."

The lump in Clay's throat shifted a little. He managed to croak out "What do you want me to do?" before it shifted again and blocked his speech. In the back of his mind, in the place where he talked to himself and kept his thoughts, he felt a kind of irritation that felt like his own voice screaming back at him. It was simultaneously revolting and familiar.

Noahleen did not tell him what to do. Instead, she looked at her hands for a long time.

Finally, she said, "I want you to let me stay home tomorrow. Trust me to text you or call you if I get into trouble. We'll put my rescue meds in an accessible place with a measured dose. I will avoid doing the laundry or going downstairs until you get home. Start with that. With my independence."

"And then?" he asked.

"Then maybe it's time for me to be in charge again," she replied. "Maybe you just need to trust me to make some of the decisions, so that you don't feel like you have to do all of it. Maybe if we do that, then you won't feel so overwhelmed that you constantly cycle back and forth between destruction and exhaustion."

"I don't know if I want that," Clay said. "I don't know if I can handle it."

"Can you handle this?" Noahleen gestured around. "Be honest with yourself."

Clay felt the scream in the back of his head intensifying as he tried to think about all the things that he would have to keep track of if he wanted to convince Noahleen not to do this thing she wanted to do. He struggled to hold on to his thoughts and to push back against it, but he could not hold onto his ideas because the scream kept getting louder and louder.

"I can't do this," he said. "I can't keep doing this."

Noahleen nodded.

"I thought about killing myself," Clay admitted. "The day I broke my hand, I was punching things because I wanted to throw myself down the stairs, but I knew it was the wrong thing to do. I stopped seeing Dr. Williams because she wanted me to talk about it, and I got the impression that she was going to use it to make me do things."

"Sometimes, people try to make you do things because they can tell that you are lost and they're trying to get you back on track," Noahleen said.

Clay shook his head. "Not her. She didn't want to listen to me, she just wanted to put me through whatever process she puts everyone through. I know this. Trust me."

"It's hard to trust you when you never tell me anything," Noahleen said. "If you'd been open with me during this whole process, then I might be able to understand things better."

"You've just got to trust me," Clay said. "I know what she was doing. She got herself assigned to assess me on the university's behalf and then she tried to have me committed for being a harm to myself."

Noahleen did not say anything back to that.

"I didn't tell you because I thought that you'd make me go inside and then we'd lose the apartment and we'd have to move back in with your parents," Clay said. "You're so... so sure about what your doctors tell you. I thought for sure you'd tell me to follow their directions and that you'd gang up on me."

Noahleen shook her head.

"No, Clay. I would have been very afraid for you, but I would have known that your doctor was not doing the right thing." Noahleen stood up and walked around the desk. She stood behind Clay's chair and massaged his shoulders and neck. "What you don't understand is that I trust my doctors because we've already fought until we understood each other. You weren't there for that. You weren't there when I had to read all about the drugs they wanted me to be on, and when I had to tell them what procedures I would and would not consent to.

"It's not your fault that you missed those things—you had to work. You had to finish school. There was no way for you to be right by my side twenty-four hours a day when I was in the hospital. My mother helped me fight that fight so that you wouldn't have to."

She dug her fingers into his shoulders hard. For a moment, Clay felt like he was going to cramp up, but then something released and he felt better.

"I need you to let me be in charge again," Noahleen said. "At least, for a little bit. I need you to trust me."

This time, Clay nodded.

"It'll be okay, you'll see," Noahleen said. "But it does mean we need to change some things. I need you to be more honest with me."

Clay nodded again.

"I can only help you reach your goals if I know what they are," Noahleen said. "That means you have to let me all the way in. You need to stop holding back."

Clay nodded once again.

"Stop nodding and tell me," Noahleen said.

Clay stopped nodding and sat up straight. He felt Noahleen's hands stop working on him as they came to rest. It felt like Noahleen was about to retreat, but she did not.

"Well?" she asked.

Visions from the mirror crept into Clay's mind again. Being thin. Having long hair again. Memories of old makeup trays and hair removal cream. Longing filled him, but terror followed closely on its heels.

The scream in his head broke out of that carefully maintained place where Clay talked to himself, cascading around the inside of his skull. He could feel his adrenaline surge as his heartbeat rocketed out of control.

Clay balled up his fists and tried to breathe. His body wanted him to bolt out of the chair and through the door. It wanted to throw itself against walls and down stairs. He told it no, but the scream moved out of his head and into his limbs, making his arms shake.

Noahleen stopped touching him. He heard her breath catch.

Clay struggled against his own body, trying to bring it back under control. He wanted to ask for help, but the lumpy terror in his throat was choking him. Noahleen held very still through the entire process, and he was thankful for that, but he was afraid that he was going to lose himself and lash out.

Finally, the lump in his throat moved to the side and Clay was able to speak.

"I don't want to pretend that we are a straight couple any more," he said. "I don't want to have to keep being male all the time." Even though he said it, Clay did not know what he meant. Those were just the words that his brain made while the scream ravaged it.

Even so, his body gave up and became still once he said it. The whole world deflated around him, too, and suddenly he felt like himself instead of feeling like he was wearing his body around and controlling it from a secret room in his head.

The scream flew out of his head into whatever sideways, not-really-real dimension it had come from.

"What does that mean?" Noahleen asked. "Are you going to leave me?"

Clay shook his head. "I don't even know."

"Well, are you going to try to get hormones? Surgery?"

Clay just shook his head again. "I like having my anatomy. I just don't like… I don't know. I want to dress differently, and I don't want people to keep talking to me about their wives and sports. I don't know. I don't want the baggage and the assumptions. I don't think I'm looking to exchange them for another set of baggage though.

"Besides," he said, "we don't have the money for me to do anything about it. Medically."

Noahleen's hands found his shoulders again. This time, she touched him like he was a stranger.

"What do you want me to do about that?" she asked.

"I don't know," Clay said. "You're the one who wanted to be in charge. You're the one who wanted to know what's been eating me."

"Yes," Noahleen said, "I am."

"What now?" he asked.

"Now, I'm going to go outside and think," Noahleen said. "Don't get up. We're okay. I just need to put some things together in my head."

Clay did not believe her, but he did not follow her out of the room either.

❖ ❖ ❖

Help Yourself

Clay held on to himself with one hand. The other was uneasily braced against the shower's wall. He could not tell which sensation was more vivid in this moment: the soothing burn of the scalding water pouring out of the showerhead and down his back, the firm but very gentle sensation of his hand lightly cupping his entire genital region against the heat from the water, or the tension in his arm as his fingers worked to maintain their hold on the slippery wall.

For just a moment, everything was perfect. The sources of his pain were clear, and he felt safe with his body and his free hand protecting the only place where he would actually mind the pain from a burn. He felt invincible there, and also electric, because for just a moment, all of his senses were communicating together. Nothing was lagging. Nothing was bleeding into pain or into ghostly flutterings in other senses. Moments like these, being so few and far-between, were more important and also more satisfying to Clay than anything.

His hand slipped against the wall. For a split second, as his weight shifted, Clay was certain that he was about to feel cold tile smacking into the back of his head. Then it was over—he was shaken, but his fingers had managed to grip the grout, and he was stable once again.

The moment was gone, though. Now, his free hand was no longer on himself, and he felt stiff in all his joints from standing in one position for too long. He shrugged it off and then reached for the handle to the faucet. It was time for him to shave and to get dressed for work.

As he stepped onto the bathmat, Clay shivered against the bracing air that wafted in from the two-inch crack where the bathroom's door had been left open to let out steam. For a second, that sensation, like the heat, seemed to bring all of his other feelings into alignment. Then it became too intense, rising in pitch until it was a biting pain. His composure went with it.

He slammed the door.

Noahleen had done what she promised. She had supported him and helped him to get ready for his accommodation meeting. She was good, too. She called attention to his behaviors when they were erratic and explained why they might distract another person, and she did not police the behaviors that were not distracting. It was a lot lower-pressure than Dr. Williams's approach.

It took a lot out of Noahleen to help him, though. Clay could see that. More than once, they had needed to stop working on things for the day because she was having too many muscle twitches to speak without tripping over herself. She started to cry then, and Clay had to reassure her that they had, in fact, done enough practicing for the day.

Neither of them had been interested in touching the other after. Most days were like this, too. The ones that were different were nice, but those days were often spent chatting on opposite sides of the apartment as they each did their own work.

That moment in the shower was the closest Clay had come to feeling sexual again since Noahleen's latest seizure cluster had started. He ached with the realization of it, but he would not have the chance to address that ache in the near term. He and Noahleen both had too much to do.

❖ ❖ ❖

Clay looked to his left, to Noahleen, as he waited for Dr. Brown and Dr. Kalkaska to arrive for their meeting. He also expected the university to send someone from Human Resources, but at this point, Clay did not know whether his expectations were realistic or not. This entire process had become hard for him to conceptualize, and it was also more drawn out than he ever would have thought it could be.

After the mess that Dr. Williams had caused when she recused herself, Human Resources had wanted to offer him free counseling through the university's counseling services. That was all. When Clay declined, they had tried to tell him that there would be no negotiation because he had declined the university's "reasonable accommodations."

Noahleen had been livid when she found out about that. It had taken her two milligrams of lorazepam and a day of being left alone to think before she was even ready to talk about what they should do next. As it turned out, though, she used that time to look up the actual Americans with Disabilities Act on the Internet.

She wrote the letter demanding that the university consider actual changes to Clay's environment and to expectations like the dress code. In it, she accused them of trying to gain control over his private medical information. She also accused them of dictating Clay's medical options to him, pointing out their refusal to discuss the matter unless he consented to a course of treatment that they had picked out.

Noahleen never once mentioned calling a lawyer or wanting to sue anyone, but something about the way she cited the relevant text from the actual law made Clay feel anxious when he signed the letter. Those words were supposed to be his, after all. If that letter had made things worse, he would not be able to blame Noahleen for it because he was the one who signed his name to her words.

She had known exactly how aggressive to be in the letter, though. It had resulted in Dr. Brown calling him in for a negotiation with the university. On the phone, Dr. Brown had mentioned that the graphic arts department was willing to make some changes on its own initiative, too, which had helped to moderate a good deal of Clay's anxiety.

Then they had started to practice. Every day. What Clay would say. What he wanted from the university. What he would settle for. Which of his behaviors were most distracting in small meetings. Which were not, and were safe for him if he felt anxious.

They also planned how they were going to get Noahleen into the room for the meeting.

Now they were here, one way or another, this issue was going to be settled. Even if Dr. Brown was not able to make good on his promises, Clay would at least have the chance to state his needs out loud. He would be able to say that the university at least knew about him and about the challenges he faced. What that meant, he did not know, but he knew that it was important. Its meaning was important to... something.

He did not have words for what he was feeling. So instead, he looked at Noahleen. He was only here because she had helped him. Guilt welled up inside him. All those months of trying to pull into himself, to be self-sufficient.... The lying about his therapy, about how things were going at work... she knew everything now. Even so, she had simply shrugged it off and helped him.

Noahleen noticed Clay watching her, and she smiled. He smiled back. She reached under the table and held his hand. When he felt her fingers inside his own, Clay shivered.

Things were going to be okay. He needed to learn from his mistakes, but he did not need to keep punishing himself for them.

That was the important thing—that he not punish himself any more.

It was not long before Dr. Kalkaska and Dr. Brown joined them in the conference room. When they walked in, they both looked surprised to see Noahleen, but they also both knew who she was. Dr. Kalkaska politely inquired about her health, and Noahleen shrugged.

"I've been sitting in on his classes," she said. "What does that tell you?"

Everyone nodded at that. None of them pushed the conversation further.

"Well, we do have some ideas that we hope you will be happy about," Dr. Brown said. "Some things we can do in the department, even if we don't get any assistance from the university administration. I would say we can talk about that, but we'll only wind up having to repeat it all once the university's representative gets here."

Clay nodded. Noahleen nodded. Dr. Kalkaska looked bored.

So they sat quietly for a moment or two. Then, the arrival of the university's Human Resources person rescued them.

"My name is Gail," she said as she took her seat. "And I know we have Dr. Kalkaska and Dr. Brown. You would be Clay, then," she stuck her hand out as she said this.

Clay shook it.

"And who are you?" Gail said to Noahleen.

"Charmed," Noahleen said, taking Gail's hand even though it was at her side. "I'm here with Clay."

Gail shook her head. "This won't do. These kinds of meetings are supposed to be confidential. Unless you are Mr. Dillon's representative, you will have to wait outside."

Clay froze. Dr. Brown frowned.

"No," Noahleen said.

Gail's brow furrowed. "I'm sorry, but you aren't allowed to be here. You don't work for the university, and even if you did, these meetings are supposed to be confidential."

Noahleen crossed her arms over her chest and sat back in her chair.

Clay felt like he should say something. "I want her here," he said. "I brought her."

Gail shrugged. She looked at him, and she shrugged. She did not say anything, though.

"It seems to me," Dr. Brown said, "that any confidentiality rules are in place to protect the privacy of Mr. Dillon during these proceedings."

Gail nodded.

"So, if he has chosen to bring someone to the meeting, then he has consented to the university sharing information with that person. There is no confidentiality issue."

"That's not how this works," Gail said.

"Why not?" Dr. Brown shot back. "The only reason why the university would have any kind of interest in shutting a member of Mr. Dillon's family out of this meeting would be to protect its own privacy, not Mr. Dillon's." He pointed his finger at Gail. "And I can promise you, even if you force her out of this room, that Mr. Dillon's family will find out exactly what happens here. They already know about your department's attempts to coerce him into compulsory therapy."

Gail, from Human Resources, sat quietly. She did not nod, but she did not argue with Dr. Brown. Instead, she seemed to shrink a little.

Noahleen uncrossed her arms and sat forward in her seat.

"Good," Dr. Brown said. "Let's get started."

Noahleen did not talk during the negotiation. That was part of the plan. She was there to support Clay, and they had already practiced what he would say over and over. She had asked him questions about his needs that they had thought the university's rep—Gail—would ask. She did not need to speak for Clay to understand what her advice would be.

Also, she was still holding his hand under the table. When she did not like what she was hearing, she dug her nails into his palm. When she wanted him to agree to something, she tickled him. Otherwise, she just squeezed whenever he started to stutter.

Slowly, Clay managed to work his way through his entire script. He told them that he was not interested in involving the university in any of the decision-making about his therapy or health care, and that he was not asking for anything but a few adjustments to existing policies. The one material benefit he was asking for, an office that he could use exclusively, was explained as a necessity because of his need for transition time between activities.

He saw Dr. Kalkaska nodding as he explained that the shared office situation actually prevented him from accomplishing anything sometimes. He walked them through the process of attempting to move from orating to grading, narrating a timeline that showed that the need to vacate his office in order to make room for the next person was disruptive to an unnecessary degree and that it created an environment wherein he simply waited until he was allowed to go home, wasting hours each week, and then worked late into the evening doing the work that he should have done during the afternoon.

At one point, Dr. Brown did break in and state that, for many full-time faculty members, what Clay was describing was actually their ideal work environment. "If that's so, then that is good for them," Clay replied, "but it is an unusual strain for me."

Noahleen squeezed his hand. He looked at her, unsure why she was interrupting him.

She nodded. Slowly and carefully, but decisively, she nodded.

Clay then explained the need that they had for a more tranquil home environment and the particular demands of having to occasionally act as the caregiver for someone who had become temporarily incapacitated. As he outlined both the ways that the stressors worked to aggravate Noahleen's condition and the ways that Noahleen's condition interacted with his ability to concentrate and to achieve his goals, he started to feel lost. Eventually, his voice slipped, and that was when she stepped in.

"The fact of the matter," Noahleen said, "is that Clay is only asking for three basic things. He is asking that the policies and deadlines of the department be laid out explicitly in any communication that is demanding input back from him. It doesn't matter whether that input is in the form of written work or participation in an event. This is something that, really, we feel is just a good professional habit, but that the university as a whole—not just this department—has traditionally failed to live up to. He's also stating—not asking—that I will be present at any performance reviews or individual meetings with supervisors. This will help to manage his anxiety and it will give him someone that he can discuss the meetings with if he needs to discuss them out loud in order to fully process them. More importantly, it gives both you and him a third party who can act as a sort of translator if either of you is confusing the other. Lastly, he wants that office. We all know you don't want to give it to him, and we know why—if he gets his own office, then it opens the door for other part-time people to make demands, and you can't accommodate everyone.

"So here's the idea: give him another job. We all know that a full-time position is off the table. If you wanted him to teach full time, you would have hired him for it already. Fine. You could give him an administrative position, part time, that serves as a pretext for him to have his own office. You already know he will deliver precise work on a deadline. Clay could use the chance to make some extra income here so that he doesn't need to take so many online courses from other schools. Meet in the middle. Do you need a webmaster for the department? It would make sense for graphic arts, of all the departments at this school, to maintain its own unique look and feel, right?"

Noahleen looked to Clay. He nodded. They had planned this, but it still felt genuine. Clay was uneasy about letting her speak for him, but they had both agreed that they needed to show the university how these accommodations would work.

Gail nodded, but she pursed her lips and closed her eyes while she did it. Clay had no idea what that meant.

Before she could speak, Dr. Kalkaska spoke up.

"What about teaching? Are you claiming that Clay needs to have your—translation? I don't know what to call it. Are you claiming he needs you to attend his classes and help him present? Or to meet with students? Because there are real issues of confidentiality that need to be worked out. Legal issues."

Clay shook his head.

"No," Noahleen said. "Clay has no trouble with his teaching duties in general. He has trouble navigating the transition from teaching and interacting with students to performing within the bureaucracy that comes with this job, and with transitioning out of work and into home life in the evening. We're not asking for anyone to hold his hand while he does his job. All we're asking for is help with the transition points. And also, you know, understanding about the fact that fielding demands from several offices at this school, demands that sometimes contradict each other is—pardon the language—it's fucking perplexing. It's frustrating enough when you aren't disabled and you haven't asked for anything special, but try doing it like we do it. Try asking for something simple, like the right to have a support person in a meeting, and being told that you have to submit to a mental health evaluation first.

"That was not only immoral and a violation of Clay's privacy, it was an avoidable barrier to his ability to function. There was no call for it. In fact, demanding it exposed the university to greater liability. So no, we're not asking that I be allowed to come in and do Clay's job, even though I'd be fully qualified to and I have worked in this field professionally before. No. We're demanding that I be allowed to observe your communications with him because your institution has a track record of breaking the law to violate Clay's rights."

When Noahleen delivered that last sentence, she narrowed her gaze at Gail. Her eyes seemed to be tunneling into the other woman's face. Gail frowned defensively.

"Fine," Gail said. "Fine. I understand what you're really saying. If the department can't offer Clay an office, we'll find him something to do in the library or we'll make him a tutor at an outreach program or something. We're a big school. There's opportunity. Unless..." she waved at Dr. Brown, "unless you do want him to do something here in the department."

Dr. Brown smiled the same kind of odd smile he had given Clay before, when he had driven Clay home from work. "I think we might, but let's see what you find for him first."

Gail frowned at that, but Dr. Kalkaska nodded.

"The other things we can do," Dr. Brown said.

Dr. Kalkaska nodded. "If you want your wife to be present at your evaluations, I don't see any reason to argue with you," she said. "It won't change anything I have to say, but so far I've only had good things to say about your teaching. As far as I'm concerned, this meeting could have been handled as an internal department matter." She cut her eyes at Gail. "It certainly would have been simpler if it had been."

Clay could not find words to express his satisfaction. He smiled and nodded though, and he squeezed Noahleen's hand under the table.

"Good," Gail said. "I'm glad that my role was ultimately unnecessary. I'll be in touch about that second part-time position."

"Good," Dr. Brown said. To Clay and Noahleen he added, "Please let me know what they find for you. I don't want this to slip through the cracks."

"Thank you," Noahleen said.

Clay nodded.

Gail excused herself.

Once she was gone and the door was closed, Dr. Brown leaned forward and rested his chin on his fist.

"So Clay becomes unvoiced? Or he just prefers to communicate differently?"

"I can talk," Clay said. "But it has a cost, when I'm trying to think carefully and make choices, I can only do one or the other. Talk or think. It makes me upset, too, sometimes, and then I just try to talk my way into getting to leave the room, even if it means giving up on a negotiation that is very important to me."

Dr. Brown nodded.

"That's what happened that day in your class, isn't it? When I was observing. You got confused and then you started typing the whole lecture into the overhead, showing the students what to do and commenting up your own code as you went."

Clay nodded.

"That's not a bad way to teach," Dr. Brown said. "I haven't seen it before, but it demonstrates how to read code comments by giving students a sense of the context under which they're created. Don't lose sight of that. You might tell yourself that it's a coping mechanism, and it might be, but it's also a very interesting approach to the material."

At that, he stood up and left. Only Dr. Kalkaska remained with them.

"Clay, you know I've been your biggest supporter," she said. "You have this job because I believe in your abilities. I never did understand why you couldn't find full-time work after you graduated—especially not with your history of successful freelance work. I get it now, and I'm sorry. I can't help thinking that if we did more with professional development—"

"Don't." Clay's voice came out hoarse. "Don't. I am grateful for all the opportunity I've had, and I've had other challenges besides my disability. I don't want to talk about them, but I will say this: Don't go thinking you could have prevented this. My inability to understand my own strengths and weaknesses was holding me back, and it was because of things that happened long before we met. You have been nothing but supportive."

"Thank you," she said. "I don't know what else to say."

Clay shrugged.

Then Dr. Kalkaska left the room, and it was just him and Noahleen.

Noahleen hugged him. "We won."

Clay felt tears running down his cheeks. He hugged her back.

"It wasn't that much of a fight," he said. "That woman from Human

Resources seemed to know that they'd fucked up hard."

"That she did," Noahleen said.

❖ ❖ ❖

Lay Down Your Burden

Dreams teeming with familiar faces crowded Clay in his sleep, as they had ever since his meeting at the university. They were not nightmares, but they did nonetheless produce stress, because the proximity of so many familiar faces was invasive. They kept pressing closer, too, and squinting as if they were examining him.

Eventually, the dreams forced him into wakefulness. Ending them was simply the only way for Clay to be alone.

In the darkness of his bedroom, Clay took deep breaths and tried to sort through his memories so that he could put names to faces. There were so many though, that he felt overwhelmed. He knew them all, and he knew that they were a mixture of faces from his past and people he had very recently had business with, but he could not identify which were which. After some time, he gave up. It was easier to let the soft blanket of the room's darkness hold him than it was to impose a wakeful analysis on the unconscious ramblings of his anxiety.

In the dark, he became acutely aware of his own body, and also of Noahleen's body lying next to him. Carefully, gently, Clay reached across the bed and slid his hand under Noahleen's blanket. His fingers found her thigh, and his entire body twitched when he made contact. For a moment, all he could do was lie still and absorb the sensation of her skin on his. The contact made his loneliness more acute, and it also gave him an awkward half-erection. Even as noncommittal and half-asleep as his arousal was, it was a strong enough sensation to overwhelm his starved nerve endings and push him into a gasping, twitching overload. It was all Clay could do to keep his legs from kicking out with the intensity of it.

His free hand traced trails down his belly, causing his erection to spring to life in anticipation of his hand.

For a moment, the world stopped. There was a barrier that he was about to cross here, and he stepped right up to it and looked at what lay on the other side while he thought about what he would do next.

If he allowed himself to do more than touch Noahleen's limbs in the dark, he would be treading into territory that he had previously always sought explicit consent to explore. It would not be the first time that she awoke in the middle of their sex, but it would be the first time that did not fall within the explicitly discussed boundaries around vacations and longer-term games of domination. It would be the first time that Clay ever truly risked rejection.

Rejection was not the only risk, either. There was always the chance that Noahleen would feel betrayed by Clay's lack of prior communication, and that this would lead to a longer-term betrayal. She had, after all, spent the last several weeks intentionally detaching herself from physical contact with him. How much of that was an aspect of treating her seizures and how much was because of her feelings toward him because of his dishonesty, Clay could not fathom. As he tried, he felt the electricity in his member fading and the torpor of sleep returning to him.

He wiggled the fingers on Noahleen's thigh, and the sensations that bloomed on the tips of his fingers faded to transparency against the dream's sensory field as it reasserted itself. Slowly, Clay let himself spread his fingers until he could feel the curve of her body. His thumb lightly worried the hollow inside her hip-bone while his fingertips settled a line across her lower abdomen, allowing his pinky to rest on hair that exuded a faint moisture and a heat that emptied Clay's chest and turned him into a vessel for single-minded longing.

With his fingers so tantalizingly deployed, Clay used his free hand on himself. He felt ashamed of doing so, but he also felt helpless to stop. He had been alone and untouched for so long and this moment, like the moment in the shower a few days ago, was unique in its lack of sensory confusion and pain. As he worked himself, Clay closed his eyes and willed his member to finish its business quickly. Instead, he felt himself drifting back into a light slumber.

Masturbating while he was almost asleep confused Clay and made his control less absolute. In the hazy space between waking and sleeping, he was hard put to track which hand was on himself and which was on Noahleen. His sense of pleasure overwhelmed his ability to differentiate the location and frequency of the individual touch causing it, and as he twisted with desire, the urgency it brought compelled him to push harder and move faster. Soon, he felt both of his hands moving, and he knew only that his own pleasure was increasing as his pinkie dug further into pubic hair and put more pressure on the tight knot of nerves that it found underneath.

Time stopped around him for a moment as his imagination fed him a brief snapshot of his hand between his own legs, fingers working furiously to dig inside himself as he let his other hand caress a hairless belly and a soft, smooth neck. He almost finished before reality asserted itself, but just before he could, Noahleen stirred beneath his hand and she reached out to him, disrupting the perfect fantasy that his imagination had asserted.

Two of her fingers found their way into his mouth and he sucked. Then her other hand closed on his wrist, moving his fingers away from her. The sense of loss that came when they were no longer in contact with her flesh was excruciating, and the entire edifice of Clay's impending orgasm seemed ready to crumble.

The crashing sense of loss this change brought on him stopped Clay's breath. Then, as quickly as she had pulled away from him, Noahleen's entire body came back. Her fingers left his mouth, taking his breath with them, but her body pushed his down, restrained his arms, and asserted itself over him. He tried to reach out for her. For any part of her—it did not matter which.

"No," she said. Then she leaned over him and took him into her mouth.

He let his fingers run through her hair, but that only made her pull away again.

"I said no," she said.

Her hands found him. He groaned. His fingers reached out.

She punched him. With a closed fist. Then, she gripped him hard, asserting her control over him and wrenching his member to make his entire body tense.

"You have a choice to make," she said. "Either you can hold still like I told you to, or you can fight me."

Clay shook his head, but he was not sure which choice he was making. When her touch became gentle again, he reached out to her, but the sudden, wrenching sensation that followed stopped him cold. Once he surrendered and let his limbs go slack, Noahleen put him back into her mouth. She barely seemed to move once she did, and Clay let himself drift as she continued to do whatever it was that he found so hard to describe.

As he accepted his own role in their encounter, the sensations she was evoking became more abstract, until he only felt that she was making him whole. Some time later, he knew it was over and that she had gone back to sleep, but he could not pinpoint the moment of transition between the two. He was elsewhere when it happened.

Clay stood before the mirror again. This time, though, he did not lean in to inspect the work he had done with the razor. There was no need to do that. The cream that he had begun to use for facial depilation did not have the problem with inconsistency that came when he used blades. Nor did it leave a dark shadow afterward to embarrass him. It took his hair down to the root and exfoliated his face in one gesture.

Clay's eyes traveled down his chest, appreciating the way that it had also removed the coarse hair that had previously hidden both his muscles and his fat. It was easier, now, to feel positive about both of them. The hair had muddied his sense of himself because he did not want it, and that feeling of loathing that he felt had bled into his feelings about his weight and about many other parts of his body. This new mode of being was better.

Noahleen's fingers curled in to his hair and pulled. He resisted until her sharp tug threatened to tear locks from his scalp, and only when he could feel tears threatening to run out of his eyes did he allow her to pull his head back. She bit his earlobe, holding on until he stopped screaming and trying to dig his fingers into the counter top.

That was the other change. Noahleen still did not want to talk about her sexual past or his, but something had shifted in their relationship to each other. Clay no longer tied her in place, nor did he hold himself tantalizingly apart from her as he played the full range of his own self-denial before allowing himself a climax. Instead, he gave himself over to her as often as he needed. Or, at least, as often as she demanded it.

Neither of them discussed Noahleen's ban on razors in the house. Instead, they worked together to groom Clay—to maintain his new hair and skin, working as a team to undo what his body had done to itself in the decade and a half since puberty.

Noahleen released Clay's ear.

"You are late for work. Stop being vain and get dressed."

He grunted a reply. She slapped him on the ass, hard.

"No talking back. You never get anything when you ask for it, anyway. Now get dressed."

He did. Now that he was hairless, it was easier. The hair removal cream kept his skin smoother, better moisturized, and more able to stand the feeling of all his clothes pressing on him constantly. It also took away that feeling of pushing and twisting that had plagued him before, since there was no longer any hair to catch the fabric and to keep it from gliding smoothly over his body.

Noahleen did not believe that this explanation for Clay's newfound comfort was the real reason why he found his work clothes so tolerable, but she also did not argue with him. Instead, she told him what she needed, and she provided... well, pain. Her discipline was hard and sometimes it was unwanted, but it was always measured and it always worked perfectly as a purgative. It left him feeling exactly as languid and fuzzy as his old episodes of self-abuse had, except that when Noahleen hurt him, there was never a chance that she would go too far. She was in control of the act, and she would not tolerate new scar tissue or broken fingers.

Clay dressed under her gaze, feeling her eyes slowly relinquishing his body to the suit he still wore like a work uniform. He suspected that she was planning their night together, but he knew that if he asked for anything, he would find that her plans only involved provoking his desire and observing its progression as it built without any hope of satisfaction. He did not want that, because she committed to the game well enough to leave him sleepless and covered in his own sweat. It did not seem to bother her in the slightest that this should happen from time to time, and he was beginning to suspect that it was integral to her own pleasure.

Once he was ready to leave for work, Clay found that Noahleen had prepared his lunch, rounded up all of his paperwork, and packed his laptop case with everything he needed. Usually, she helped him with these things. Today, he realized, he really must have let himself linger for too long in the bathroom.

She let him kiss her on the cheek before he left, but briefly and chastely. As he stepped past her, though, he felt her hand playing over the small of his back and lingering to cup his ass, and he sighed.

She was planning something, she just refused to say what.

❖ ❖ ❖

Class Discussion

Clay smiled out at the sea of faces in his classroom. There were more than forty of them this semester, and they were all shifting uncomfortably, the way that people always did on the first day of class. The first day was always a good day for him, but especially so today. This particular first day of class felt safe not only because he had rehearsed it so many times before, but also because he was finally in control of his own comfort and security. His clothes were loose and comfortable, his laptop held a queued presentation that he could type over and pause to talk through. This way, he would not have to try to maintain his performance for an uninterrupted ninety minutes.

All of that made it easier to do what he had to do next. That was not to say, though, that what he had to do next would be easy. Doing new things was never easy for Clay. This seemed easier, though, than the way he had started the semester before, and it promised to make the entire process easier than it had been when he was toiling away in isolation.

He looked at the clock. It said 2:01. Time to start class.

Clay stepped forward. At first, he tried to look into the glare of the track lights, but then he remembered that he had left the stage lighting off and the room lighting up to full. He was going to have to do this while looking at all of his students. Panic started in the back of his throat and then spread out to his fingertips. Instinctively, he let his wrists go limp and shook his hands. The panic dissipated.

He could do this.

"Hi everyone," he started, "and welcome to CSS level one. If you're with me, then you have completed HTML one and Basic Applications. Is there anyone here that has not completed both of those courses?"

He paused and looked around the room. No hands went up.

"Good," he said, "then let's move forward. My name is Clay Dillon, and I will be your instructor for the next fifteen weeks. Before we get started, you should know a little bit about me. I'm a graduate of this university, for starters. I have a master's degree in the graphic arts, and before I started teaching, I enjoyed a successful freelance career as a web designer and logo artist. If you have any questions about that kind of work, you'll find my office hours on the syllabus."

It felt good to be moving through his speech so smoothly, but as Clay approached the end of his introduction, he felt the panic coming back. Under his clothes, a thousand pinpricks started up in the places where his body hair had been. For the briefest moment, he considered excusing himself to the restroom until his sensory difficulties passed.

Then he remembered Noahleen's smile. She was planning something. All he had to do was complete his first day of class, and then he would be able to give himself up to her. She would listen to him talk about the problems he was having now, and he would tell her how he managed to squash his anxiety. He would tell her about the importance of this exact moment, and then (if he wanted), she would allow him to stop making decisions for the rest of the night.

Images raced through Clay's head. They all related to the things that Noahleen did to him when he stopped making decisions. His panic went away, and none of the students were staring at him any more than usual, so he assumed that it must have only lasted for a second or two. He continued his speech.

"In this class, we will be using a combination of lectures, activities, and example code delivered through a multitude of technological aides. You'll see me silently mark up code in response to your questions, and you'll be asked to produce working templates and to design modifications to existing pages yourselves. All of this is only possible when we have open, clear communication. That's why I'm telling you now, on the first day, that I am autistic."

As the words left his mouth, it felt like his whole body was exhaling. Whatever these students did in response to his disclosure, he was past the point of being able to help it. Strangely, it felt just like surrendering himself to Noahleen did. They might mistreat him, but at least he had made the decision to open himself up to that. If they complained about him now, they would have to deal with what he was and what that meant. They could not simply dismiss his tics as poor self-control, and they could not tell him that he was performing emotions that he did not feel. The word "autistic" protected him from that. It might open him up to new kinds of abuse in the long run, but Clay felt he could tolerate that. He just did not want anyone imposing their inferences about his motivations and behavior on him any more.

Trembling and hoping not to show it, Clay surrendered to the moment and let himself speak off-script.

"Normally, this is not something that affects my teaching. Sometimes, though, my senses simply don't behave. On those days, I might be dizzy, or I might be overly sensitive to sound. Please bear with me if that happens, because one of the other problems I have is that I have to work very hard to maintain my tone of voice. When I'm also experiencing sensory distress, I often lose control over the volume and tone of my vocal performance. Sometimes, I even lose the ability to speak for short periods of time.

"Know that if this happens, I'm not trying to be snide or sarcastic. I promise I won't do that, and if you think you hear it, you can let me know so that I can try to stop doing it. Just please don't draw the wrong conclusions. If you promise not to assume I'm being a dick, then I promise to not be one. That's all this really comes down to."

A few people giggled. Some others nodded. Some of the ones that nodded looked a bit sad, but Clay tried not to focus on that. Instead, he pulled out his smart phone and turned the screen on. The projector sprang to life with his phone screen, and he started to touch-type. As he did, the words were projected onto the room's presentation screen:

If I become unvoiced, I will continue to lecture, but you might have to cope with the speed of my typing. Generally, I do actually type faster than you'd want me to speak. When I'm distressed, though, that might change.

The good news is, if I'm having a bad day, then you basically get all the notes on the projector and you can copy them at your own pace. The bad news is that I won't be as effective during a question-and-answer period when I have to do this. It's difficult for me to leave my prepared speech when I'm already in distress.

Sometimes, I will do this when I'm not distressed. Mostly, it will be to answer questions with in-line comments on demonstrations of the various techniques you are here to learn.

I know this is a lot to take in, but understanding my work process is going to be integral to our success together in the classroom. I look forward to working with all of you. Now, if you please, let's move into the syllabus.

First: Any questions?

Hands shot up around the room.

Clay smiled and pointed to the first one he saw, off in the corner in the back, near the fire exit. The hand belonged to a small blonde woman whose eyes were lost in the shadows of the room's lighting.

"Is it okay to text message you? Like, if we have questions or if we need to talk to you? Or do you only want phone calls?"

He typed.

Go ahead and text me. I don't think it's a secret that text is going to be better for me at this point.

He pointed to another hand. This time, it was a question about how old he'd been when he was diagnosed. After that, it was about whether or not he thought that creative technological jobs had a special appeal to autistic people. Then there was one about whether or not his sensory issues ever escalated into vertigo.

After a point, Clay stopped trying to text his answers to the screen and started answering verbally. He switched the projector over so that he could control it from his laptop, intending to display the syllabus so that he could transition into the business of the day.

As soon as his phone disconnected from the projector, he received a text message.

It said, *Thank you. I am also autistic, and I have trouble listening and controlling the tone of my voice too.*

While Clay answered more questions, the texts kept coming. The first two both came from the same person, the person who had texted him disclosing that she was autistic as well:

I was shocked that you told the class, she said, *all through school, they tried to convince us that we had to blend in, that the goal was to overcome the way we are.*

And then: *You are proof that they are bullshit.*

That last text shocked Clay. Not because of the language, but because he had not intended to prove anything. He was just trying to get through his day without losing his job or his mind. A text from another number came in while Clay was reading the three from the first person.

I've been trying to get accommodations from the student disability services, but they are assholes. Can you help?

He looked around the room, wondering who had sent this most recent message, and his phone alert went off again.

I was going back and forth about whether or not to ask you for extra test time because of my ADD. Thank you for making me feel comfortable about it.

Another unfamiliar number. Before Clay had a chance to wonder about it, though, there were more.

I'm not autistic, but I'm glad you're telling people you are. I remember how hard it was to tell everyone I'm gay.

Clay kept looking around the room. He realized that he had stopped looking for questions because of the flood of text messages. As he surveyed his class, he saw students staring down at the devices in their laps. It was hard to tell who was texting and who was taking advantage of the opportunity to play with their phones.

His text message alert went off again. And again.

He silenced it and gestured to the projector.

"We have to cover the syllabus before we run out of time, but I want you all to know that I'm going to respond to your messages during my office time. Please do me a favor, though—put your first name in your text for me so that I have some idea who I'm talking to."

Around the room, he saw nods. Clay looked at his phone one last time before he started narrating the course syllabus. The most recent message he saw said simply: *It's about damn time. You wouldn't believe how many of us there are, but no one wants to talk about it.* It was from the same number that had started the wave of texts.

Smiling, Clay pocketed his phone and focused on finishing his work.

"This course syllabus contains all of the basic requirements for all of the major projects in this class. You won't be able to finish the work in those projects without the handouts I'll give you to work with, but this at least lets you see a list of tasks and a copy of the rubric that will be used to judge your work.

"Now," he said, "we won't make it there today, but generally speaking, you can count on the last half of each class taking place in the computer lab. This is because designing web sites is a technique-based skill. You can't just memorize the tags, you have to create something. You only get better with practice."

He scrolled down to display the location of the computer lab.

"This is the room that is booked for our course's computer time. It will be the same all semester."

His phone vibrated against his thigh. Someone was still talking to him.

For once, Clay looked forward to his office time.

❖ ❖ ❖

Transitional Thoughts

Clay stood before the mirror with a razor in his hand. After two months of using the cream, it had stopped removing his hair and started causing his face and stomach to break out. At first, Noahleen had been reluctant to allow him to use a razor again, but Clay assured her that there was no longer any danger in it. What he had needed from razor blades was something that Noahleen's newfound taste for control now supplied. It had taken her a couple of weeks to appreciate this, but as his rash grew worse and his hair reasserted itself, she slowly came around to the necessity of his shaving again.

This time, as Clay regarded his body, he felt no recriminations. His skin was softer, more healthy, and more... *right*... than it had been since he was fifteen. Even with coarse black stubble scratching at the palms of his hands as he rubbed himself down with the shaving soap, the satisfaction he received from putting his hands on his own body was greater than anything he could remember feeling as an adult. Or it almost was. His mind drifted to Noahleen's untender discipline as he found a jagged scab from her latest experiment, a new use of the razor that required far more trust and far more control than Clay had thought either of them was capable of.

There was no bite to the razor's scrape as it moved across his belly. The shaving soap Clay had ordered for his body work was good, and the new razors he had found for the job were even better. It had taken some time for him to screw up the courage to actually ask for advice about this project, but there was safety in anonymity, and he found many places online where he could ask for help.

Finishing his belly, Clay lathered his legs, which were still damp from his shower. Oddly enough, his legs were the challenge for him. Shaving his belly was always easy, and he had no trouble navigating the crevices of his genitalia with the razor—he had, in fact, not even had a nick or a bit of razor burn around his perineum or scrotum, not even on his first attempt. His legs, though, always bled. He never felt the cuts as he made them, but after he finished he always found a few places where the blood flowed freely.

He did his best, though, each time. He shaved slowly, with the grain, and made two passes, applying new shaving soap in between each one. In the end, blood or no blood, his legs were perfectly smooth, their muscles more clearly defined, and the skin covering them looked healthier.

There was a knock on the door that just happened to coincide with Clay's attempt to shave around his ankle, and it startled him, so of course he nicked himself. As Clay attempted to staunch the absurdly fast flow of blood from the minuscule nick above his heel, he heard his brother's voice booming through the door.

"Hey, uh, sorry to interrupt. I was just wanting to say thanks before

I headed out to work. You've been great all week, and I wanted to offer to take you out to eat tonight. As a thanks."

"Sure!" Clay shouted through the door. It was hard to make himself heard, bent over as he was and with the sink running. He tried, though. "Why tonight, though?"

"Oh, I'm going home tonight," A.J. shouted. "We have about a half day of work to do, and then our project is over. I just wanted to thank you properly before I left."

"Okay! Great!" Clay felt himself running out of steam. He could not finish his shave until his brother left him alone, and he was still bent over, holding toilet paper to his heel, and hoping that the nick would stop bleeding soon.

After a few seconds of silence, he assumed that A.J. had left for the day. His brother's presence on his couch for the last week had been a challenge, a true test of Clay's ability to endure denial and to fuel himself on promises of future gratification. It had been impossible to indulge himself properly with a guest sleeping in the living room, and beside that, his brother's straitlaced parochialism had made Clay reluctant to parade around the house in a state of undress that would have revealed the recent changes to his body.

The nick over his heel stopped bleeding, and Clay finished his shave. Afterward, he rubbed Bag Balm over his entire body. Noahleen detested the smell of it, so he only used it when he would be leaving the house for the day. It was the best thing he had found for both razor burn and for moisturizing his skin. It felt like Vaseline going on, but it made everything that it touched plump, soft, and unbelievably smooth. Clay chalked that up to the lanolin in the balm. It smelled vaguely like a barn, but his skin just drank it up.

As Clay worked it into the places where his legs met his body, he regarded himself in the mirror again. He had never imagined that he would be truly happy with his body, let alone that he would find a way to embrace the enlarged biceps and pectoral muscles that age and exercise had forced on him, but as he looked at his own genitals, he realized that if a penis could be made into something that was not necessarily masculine on its own, then mere muscles were no real challenge to him. In fact, after having conditioned his skin over the course of months, they no longer even seemed to be necessarily masculine features on their own.

After he finished, Clay washed his hands and went to work on his hair. His sensitivities required that it remain short, but he had found a

style that, with the liberal application of styling paste, sat halfway
between a flat-top and a pixie cut. It seemed to fit his new sense of
himself perfectly, and it had not broken Noahleen's rule about
maintaining his persona and presentation in the workplace. It had,
however, adequately softened his features so that he felt more
comfortable with himself when others looked at him.

With his hair fully styled and his body groomed, Clay took one last
look in the mirror. It was evident that if his pecs grew just a little while
becoming more heavy, he could pass for an intentionally butch woman.
At least from the waist up, he could. He was proud of that. Still, when
he thought of himself, he still thought in terms of male pronouns and
masculine roles. Or, mostly he did. At the grocery store he had been
"ma'am"ed a few times, and every time it happened he felt flattered.
Still, in his head, he used masculine terms to talk to himself.

There were not words for what he felt about that, but he no longer
felt the out of body sensations that had preoccupied him for as long as
he could remember. Instead, he lived with a tinkerer's sense of
satisfaction, feeling that he had already done better than others would
have thought he could, but knowing he would continue making small
adjustments for as long as he lived.

Now that his grooming ritual was discharged, his mind wandered
back to his brother's visit.

It had seemed practical at the outset. A.J. worked in construction,
mostly doing renovation work, and he had a job in town and needed a
place to stay. The brothers had not spent a night under the same roof
since they were teens, but it had seemed natural to save A.J. the cost of
the hotel, and he had been a fairly innocuous guest. Over the course of
the week, though, the visit had turned heavy, and Clay could see that
his brother was concerned for and about him. More than once, he
pointed out the fact that Clay was doing so well now, and when he did,
he pointed out the infrequency of Clay's visits home.

At first, Clay thought that A.J. was angling for him to reconcile
with their father Mark, but surprisingly, that had not been his
intention. Instead, A.J. pushed him to contact their mother, Kitty. He
made a persuasive case for it, pointing out her success at managing her
mental health conditions and her recent remarriage as signs that she
was now stable enough to maintain a healthy relationship with her
children.

It had been hard to listen to—Clay had not interacted with their
mother since he was fifteen, and the terror and loathing that had

initially driven him away from her had only grown in the decade and a half that they had remained apart. Still, something in A.J.'s appeal had touched Clay, and his natural sense of curiosity about the fate of his family members had been aroused.

He was still unsure about whether he would go through with A.J.'s request or not. His brother had admitted to the continued over-emphasis of religion in their mother's life, and that gave Clay pause. Kitty's hallucinations about end times and her delusional conversations with the disembodied voices of various saints had provoked her most terrifying and violent episodes during his childhood.

Going back to see her would be quite the adjustment.

In the mirror, the softened edges of his face and the plump fullness of his skin screamed at him. How could he work so hard to accentuate the features that he knew full well he shared with his mother, all while refusing to make room for her in his life?

Just as importantly, though, was the question of how she would react once it became apparent that he came not as a successful son looking for reconciliation, but as an unabashedly queer autistic. What would she say about his rebellion against the traditional notions of domesticity, when he was accentuating by his persistent commitment to what looked, for all intents and purposes, to be a heterosexual marriage?

Except, after six months of work, he and Noahleen no longer looked like they were in a heterosexual marriage. People knew *something* had changed, even if none of them seemed to have words to describe what it was. Clay could tell that just by watching them search for ways to start conversations with Noahleen when she came out to social functions within the department.

A conviction took hold in Clay's mind just then. He was still unsure whether he would contact Kitty or not, but he knew one thing for certain—he was finally going to tell A.J. that he was autistic. Clay would not let his brother go home without doing that one thing to ensure that they knew one another better.

After that, perhaps it was time to force Noahleen to confront the idea that their days of presenting Clay Dillon to the world as unchanged, straight, and male were almost up. She could not deny, after all, that his changes were not only picking up speed but also becoming more pronounced.

Clay wondered what she would do, though, if the changes stopped happening at her speed and under her control.

❖ ❖ ❖

About the Author

I'm performing naked in public with a ski mask on,
skinning myself in slow motion.
I walk around, leaving meaty footprints
on the carpet, making messes of myself
in front of extended relatives
and re-enacting rituals with razor blades
in excruciating patterns with unsteady hands.

My face finds itself perpetually surprised,
taking in defiance and acknowledging regret,
yet still demanding smiles carved out of eloquence.
Locked into my contracted attitude,
it sublimates months-long performances in
orgies observers assume are rehearsed to virtuosity.

The reality of the spectacle,
all meaty sinew and dangling genital
made anonymous under pretense,
is that there is more truth in this ballet
than in anything my therapist might say;
more reward from rubbernecked gawkers
who can't stop watching me change
than I could find in an embrace.

When the lights go down, eyes no longer play
upon the inside of my skin. I nearly faint.
So much of my essence is bled away.
I am more alive, though,
for the feeling of being drained,
and I stagger into the wall on my way to the door
to avoid falling sideways onto my feet
and face-first into the floor.

Now I'm reviewing my bits,
seeking improvements,
and utterly failing to find my cover

before the curtain rises again.
I'm nothing but a panting mess.
One act down, but still under your stares,
I strike a pose. It's already time to begin
another performance.

Clearing my throat, I declare:
Welcome to *Imaginary Friends*.

- M. Monje

Defiant is the twenty-fifth book in the Shaping Clay series. *Nothing is Right* was the first. Number twenty-six will appear after *Imaginary Friends, Gaslight Village,* and *Dancing Star: The Early Life of Kitty Dillon* (Numbers 2-4).

CPSIA information can be obtained at www.ICGtesting.com
Printed in the USA
LVOW04s1324250615

443861LV00023B/258/P